GWENDY'S
BUTTON BOX

GWENDY'S BUTTON BOX

STEPHEN KING AND RICHARD CHIZMAR

CEMETERY DANCE PUBLICATIONS
BALTIMORE, MARYLAND
2017

Cemetery Dance Publications
132B Industry Lane, Unit #7
Forest Hill, MD 21050
www.cemeterydance.com

First Edition ★ Third Printing ★ June 2017

ISBN: 978-1-58767-610-9

Cover Artwork © 2017 by Ben Baldwin
Interior Artwork © 2017 by Keith Minnion
Interior Design © 2017 by Desert Isle Design, LLC

1

THERE ARE THREE WAYS up to Castle View from the town of Castle Rock: Route 117, Pleasant Road, and the Suicide Stairs. Every day this summer—yes, even on Sundays—twelve-year-old Gwendy Peterson has taken the stairs, which are held by strong (if time-rusted) iron bolts and zig-zag up the cliffside. She walks the first hundred, jogs the second hundred, and forces herself to run up the last hundred and five, pelting—as her father would say—hellbent for election. At the top she bends over, red-faced, clutching her knees, hair in sweaty clumps against her cheeks (it always escapes her ponytail on that last sprint, no matter how tight she ties it), and puffing like an old carthorse. Yet there has been some improvement. When she straightens up and looks down the length of her body, she can see the tips of her sneakers. She couldn't do that in June, on the last day of school, which also happened to be her last day in Castle Rock Elementary.

Her shirt is sweat-pasted to her body, but on the whole, she feels pretty good. In June, she felt ready to die of a heart attack every time she reached the top. Nearby, she can hear the shouts of the kids on the playground. From a bit farther away comes the chink of an aluminum bat hitting a baseball as the Senior League kids practice for the Labor Day charity game.

She's wiping her glasses on the handkerchief she keeps in the pocket of her shorts for just that purpose when she is addressed. "Hey, girl. Come on over here for a bit. We ought to palaver, you and me."

Gwendy puts her specs on and the blurred world comes back into focus. On a bench in the shade, close to the gravel path leading from the stairs into the Castle View Recreational Park, sits a man in black jeans, a black coat like for a suit, and a white shirt unbuttoned at the top. On his head is a small neat black hat. The time will come when Gwendy has nightmares about that hat.

The man has been on this same bench every day this week, always reading the same book (*Gravity's Rainbow*, it's thick and looks mighty arduous), but has

8

never said anything to her until today. Gwendy regards him warily.

"I'm not supposed to talk to strangers."

"That's good advice." He looks about her father's age, which would make him thirty-eight or so, and not bad looking, but wearing a black suit coat on a hot August morning makes him a potential weirdo in Gwendy's book. "Probably got it from your mother, right?"

"Father," Gwendy says. She'll have to go past him to get to the playground, and if he really is a weirdo he might try to grab her, but she's not too worried. It's broad daylight, after all, the playground is close and well-populated, and she's got her wind back.

"In that case," says the man in the black coat, "let me introduce myself. I'm Richard Farris. And you are—?"

She debates, then thinks, what harm? "Gwendy Peterson."

"So there. We know each other."

Gwendy shakes her head. "Names aren't knowing."

He throws back his head and laughs. It's totally charming in its honest good humor, and Gwendy can't help smiling. She still keeps her distance, though.

He points a finger-gun at her: pow. "That's a good one. *You're* a good one, Gwendy. And while we're at it, what kind of name is that, anyway?"

"A combination. My father wanted a Gwendolyn—that was his granny's name—and my mom wanted a Wendy, like in *Peter Pan*. So they compromised. Are you on vacation, Mr. Farris?" This seems likely; they are in Maine, after all, and Maine proclaims itself Vacationland. It's even on the license plates.

"You might say so. I travel here and there. Michigan one week, Florida the next, then maybe a hop to Coney Island for a Redhot and a ride on the Cyclone. I am what you might call a rambling man, and America is my beat. I keep an eye on certain people, and check back on them every once and again."

Chink goes the bat on the field past the playground, and there are cheers.

"Well, it's been nice talking to you, Mr. Farris, but I really ought to—"

"Stay a bit longer. You see, you're one of the people I've been keeping an eye on just recently."

This should sound sinister (and does, a little), but he's still smiling in the aftermath of his laughter, his eyes are lively, and if he's Chester the Molester, he's keeping it well hidden. Which, she supposes, the best ones would do. Step into my parlor, said the spider to the fly.

"I've got a theory about you, Miss Gwendy Peterson. Formed, as all the best theories are, by close observation. Want to hear it?"

"Sure, I guess."

"I notice you are a bit on the plump side."

Maybe he sees her tighten up at that, because he raises a hand and shakes his head, as if to say *not so fast*.

"You might even think of yourself as fat, because girls and women in this country of ours have strange ideas about how they look. The media...do you know what I mean by the media?"

"Sure. Newspapers, TV, *Time* and *Newsweek*."

"Nailed it. So okay. The media says, 'Girls, women, you can be anything you want to be in this brave new world of equality, as long as you can still see your toes when you stand up straight.'"

He *has* been watching me, Gwendy thinks, because I do that every day when I get to the top. She blushes. She can't help it, but the blush is a surface thing. Below it is a kind of so-what defiance. It's what got her going on the stairs in the first place. That and Frankie Stone.

"My theory is that somebody tweaked you about your weight, or how you look, or both, and you decided to take the matter in hand. Am I close? Maybe not a bullseye, but at least somewhere on the target?"

Perhaps because he's a stranger, she finds herself able to tell him what she hasn't confided to either of her parents. Or maybe it's his blue eyes, which are curious and interested but with no meanness in them—at least not that she can see. "This kid at school, Frankie Stone, started calling me Goodyear. You know, like—"

"Like the blimp, yes, I know the Goodyear Blimp."

"Uh-huh. Frankie's a puke." She thinks of telling the man how Frankie goes strutting around the playground, chanting *I'm Frankie Stoner! Got a two-foot boner!* and decides not to.

"Some of the other boys started calling me that, and then a few of the girls picked it up. Not my friends, other girls. That was sixth grade. Middle school starts next month, and…well…"

"You've decided that particular nickname isn't going to follow you there," says Mr. Richard Farris. "I see. You'll also grow taller, you know." He eyes her up and down, but not in a way she finds creepy. It's more scientific. "I'm thinking you might top out around five-ten or -eleven before you're done. Tall, for a girl."

"Started already," Gwendy says, "but I'm not going to wait."

"All pretty much as I thought," Farris says. "Don't wait, don't piss and moan, just attack the issue. Go head-on. Admirable. Which is why I wanted to make your acquaintance."

"It's been nice talking to you, Mr. Farris, but I have to go now."

12

"No. You need to stay right here." He's not smiling anymore. His face is stern, and the blue eyes seem to have gone gray. The hat lays a thin line of shadow over his brow, like a tattoo. "I have something for you. A gift. Because you are the one."

"I don't take things from strangers," Gwendy says. Now she's feeling a little scared. Maybe more than a little.

"Names aren't knowing, I agree with you there, but we're not strangers, you and I. I know you, and I know this thing I have was made for someone like you. Someone who is young and set solidly on her feet. I felt you, Gwendy, long before I saw you. And here you are." He moves to the end of the bench and pats the seat. "Come sit beside me."

Gwendy walks to the bench, feeling like a girl in a dream. "Are you...Mr. Farris, do you want to hurt me?"

He smiles. "Grab you? Pull you into the bushes and perhaps have my wicked way with you?" He points across the path and forty feet or so up it. There, two or three dozen kids wearing Castle Rock Day Camp t-shirts are playing on the slides and swings and monkey bars while four camp counselors watch over them. "I don't think I'd get away with that, do you? And besides, young girls don't interest me sexually.

They don't interest me at all, as a rule, but as I've already said—or at least implied—you are different. Now sit down."

She sits. The sweat coating her body has turned cold. She has an idea that, despite all his fine talk, he will now try to kiss her, and never mind the playground kids and their teenage minders just up the way. But he doesn't. He reaches under the bench and brings out a canvas bag with a drawstring top. He pulls it open and removes a beautiful mahogany box, the wood glowing a brown so rich that she can glimpse tiny red glints deep in its finish. It's about fifteen inches long, maybe a foot wide, and half that deep. She wants it at once, and not just because it's a beautiful thing. She wants it because it's *hers*. Like something really valuable, really loved, that was lost so long ago it was almost forgotten but is now found again. Like she owned it in another life where she was a princess, or something.

"What is it?" Gwendy asks in a small voice.

"A button box," he says. "Your button box. Look."

He tilts it so she can see small buttons on top of the box, six in rows of two, and a single at each end. Eight in all. The pairs are light green and dark green, yellow and orange, blue and violet. One of the end-buttons is red. The other is black. There's also a small lever at each end of the box, and what looks like a slot in the middle.

"The buttons are very hard to push," says Farris. "You have to use your thumb, and put some real muscle into it. Which is a good thing, believe me. Wouldn't want to make any mistakes with those, oh no. Especially not with the black one."

Gwendy has forgotten to feel afraid of the man. She's fascinated by the box, and when he hands it to her, she takes it. She was expecting it to be heavy—mahogany is a heavy wood, after all, plus who knows what might be inside—but it's not. She could bounce it up and down on her tented fingers. Gwendy runs a finger over the glassy, slightly convex surface of the buttons, seeming to almost feel the colors lighting up her skin.

"Why? What do they do?"

"We'll discuss them later. For now, direct your attention to the little levers. They're much easier to pull than the buttons are to push; your little finger is enough. When you pull the one on the left end—next to the red button—it will dispense a chocolate treat in the shape of an animal."

"I don't—" Gwendy begins.

"You don't take candy from strangers, I know," Farris says, and rolls his eyes in a way that makes her giggle. "Aren't we past that, Gwendy?"

15

"It's not what I was going to say. I don't eat *choco-late*, is what I was going to say. Not this summer. How will I ever lose any weight if I eat candy? Believe me, once I start, I can't stop. And chocolate is the worst. I'm like a chocoholic."

"Ah, but that's the beauty of the chocolates the button box dispenses," says Richard Farris. "They are small, not much bigger than jelly beans, and very sweet…but after you eat one, you won't want another. You'll want your meals, but not seconds on anything. And you won't want any other treats, either. Especially those late-night waistline killers."

Gwendy, until this summer prone to making herself Fluffernutters an hour or so before bedtime, knows exactly what he's talking about. Also, she's always starving after her morning runs.

"It sounds like some weird diet product," she says. "The kind that stuffs you up and then makes you pee like crazy. My granny tried some of that stuff, and it made her sick after a week or so."

"Nope. Just chocolate. But *pure*. Not like a candy-bar from the store. Try it."

She debates the idea, but not for long. She curls her pinky around the lever—it's too small to operate easily with any of the others—and pulls. The slot opens. A narrow wooden shelf slides out. On it is a chocolate rabbit, no bigger than a jellybean, just as Mr. Farris said.

She picks it up and looks at it with amazed wonder. "Wow. Look at the *fur*. The *ears*! And the cute little *eyes*."

"Yes," he agrees. "A beautiful thing, isn't it? Now pop it in! Quick!"

Gwendy does so without even thinking about it, and sweetness floods her mouth. He's right, she never tasted a Hershey bar this good. She can't remember ever having tasted *anything* this good. That gorgeous flavor isn't just in her mouth; it's in her whole head. As it melts on her tongue, the little shelf slides back in, and the slot closes.

"Good?" he asks.

"Mmm." It's all she can manage. If this were ordinary candy, she'd be like a rat in a science experiment, working that little lever until it broke off or until the dispenser stopped dispensing. But she doesn't want another. And she doesn't think she'll be stopping for a Slushee at the snack bar on the far side of the playground, either. She's not hungry at all. She's...

"Are you satisfied?" Farris asks.

"Yes!" That's the word, all right. She has never been so satisfied with anything, not even the two-wheeler she got for her ninth birthday.

"Good. Tomorrow you'll probably want another one, and you can *have* another one if you do, because you'll have the button box. It's your box, at least for now."

"How many chocolate animals are inside?"

Instead of answering her question, he invites her to pull the lever at the other end of the box.

"Does it give a different kind of candy?"

"Try it and see."

She curls her pinky around the small lever and pulls it. This time when the shelf slides out of the slot, there's a silver coin on it, so large and shiny she has to squint against the morning light that bounces off it. She picks it up and the shelf slides back in. The coin is heavy in her hand. On it is a woman in profile. She's wearing what looks like a tiara. Below her is a semi-circle of stars, interrupted by the date: 1891. Above her are the words *E Pluribis Unum.*

"That is a Morgan silver dollar," Farris tells her in a lecturely voice. "Almost half an ounce of pure silver. Created by Mr. George Morgan, who was just thirty years old when he engraved the likeness of Anna Willess Williams, a Philadelphia matron, to go on what you'd call the 'heads' side of the coin. The American Eagle is on the tails side."

"It's beautiful," she breathes, and then—with huge reluctance—she holds it out to him.

Farris crosses his hands on his chest and shakes his head. "It's not mine, Gwendy. It's yours. Everything that comes out of the box is yours—the candy and the coins—because the *box* is yours. The current numismatic value of that Morgan dollar is just shy of six hundred dollars, by the way."

"I...I can't take it," she says. Her voice is distant in her own ears. She feels (as she did when she first started her runs up the Suicide Stairs two months ago) that she may faint. "I didn't do anything to earn it."

"But you will." From the pocket of his black jacket he takes an old-fashioned pocket watch. It shoots more arrows of sun into Gwendy's eyes, only these are gold instead of silver. He pops up the cover and consults the face within. Then he drops it back into his pocket. "My time is short now, so look at the buttons and listen closely. Will you do that?"

"Y-yes."

"First, put the silver dollar in your pocket. It's distracting you."

She does as he says. She can feel it against her thigh, a heavy circle.

"How many continents in the world, Gwendy? Do you know?"

"Seven," she says. They learned that in third or fourth grade.

"Exactly. But since Antarctica is for all practical purposes deserted, it isn't represented here... except, of course, by the black button, and we'll get to that." One after another, he begins to lightly tap the convex surfaces of the buttons that are in pairs. "Light green: Asia. Dark green: Africa. Orange: Europe. Yellow: Australia. Blue: North America. Violet: South America. Are you with me? Can you remember?"

"Yes." She says it with no hesitation. Her memory has always been good, and she has a crazy idea that the wonderful piece of candy she ate is further aiding her concentration. She doesn't know what all this means, but can she remember which color represents which continent? Absolutely. "What's the red one?"

"Whatever you want," he says, "and you *will* want it, the owner of the box always does. It's normal. Wanting to know things and do things is what the human race is all about. Exploration, Gwendy! Both the disease and the cure!"

I'm no longer in Castle Rock, Gwendy thinks. *I've entered one of those places I like to read about. Oz or Narnia or Hobbiton. This can't be happening.*

"Just remember," he continues, "the red button is the only button you can use more than once."

"What about the black one?"

"It's everything," Farris says, and stands up. "The whole shebang. The big kahuna, as your father would say."

She looks at him, saucer-eyed. Her father *does* say that. "How do you know my fath—"

"Sorry to interrupt, very impolite, but I really have to go. Take care of the box. It gives gifts, but they're small recompense for the responsibility. And be careful. If your parents found it, there would be questions."

"Oh my God, would there ever," Gwendy says, and utters a breathless whisper of a laugh. She feels punched in the stomach. "Mr. Farris, why did you give this to me? *Why me?*"

"Stashed away in this world of ours," Farris says, looking down at her, "are great arsenals of weapons that could destroy all life on this planet for a million years. The men and women in charge of them ask themselves that same question every day. It is you because you were the best choice of those in this place at this time. Take care of the box. I advise you not to let *anyone* find it, not just your parents, because people are curious. When they see a lever, they want to pull it. And when they see a button, they want to push it."

"But what happens if they do? What happens if *I* do?"

Richard Farris only smiles, shakes his head, and starts toward the cliff, where a sign reads: BE CAREFUL! CHILDREN UNDER 10 UNACCOMPANIED BY ADULT *NOT ALLOWED!* Then he turns back. "Say! Why do they call them the Suicide Stairs, Gwendy?"

"Because a man jumped from them in 1934, or something like that," she says. She's holding the button box on her lap. "Then a woman jumped off four or five years ago. My dad says the city council talked about taking them down, but everyone on the council is Republican, and Republicans hate change. That's what my dad says, anyway. One of them said the stairs are a tourist attraction, which they sort of are, and that one suicide every thirty-five years or so wasn't really so terrible. He said if it became a fad, they'd take another vote."

Mr. Farris smiles. "Small towns! Gotta love them!"

"I answered your question, now you answer mine! What happens if I push one of these buttons? What happens if I push the one for Africa, for instance?" And as soon as her thumb touches the dark green button, she feels an urge—not strong, but appreciable—to push it and find out for herself.

His smile becomes a grin. Not a terribly nice one, in Gwendy Peterson's opinion. "Why ask what you already know?"

Before she can say another word, he's started down the stairs. She sits on the bench for a moment, then gets up, runs to the rusty iron landing, and peers down. Although Mr. Farris hasn't had time enough to get all the way to the bottom—nowhere near—he's gone. Or almost. Halfway down, about a hundred and fifty iron steps, his small neat black hat lies either abandoned or blown off.

She goes back to the bench and puts the button box—*her* button box—in the canvas drawstring bag, then descends the stairs, holding the railing the whole way. When she reaches the little round hat, she considers picking it up, then kicks it over the side instead, watching it fall, flipping over all the way to the bottom to land in the weeds. When she comes back later that day, it's gone.

This is August 22nd, 1974.

2

HER MOM AND DAD both work, so when Gwendy gets back to the little Cape Cod on Carbine Street, she has it to herself. She puts the button box under her bed and leaves it there for all of ten minutes before realizing that's no good. She keeps her room reasonably neat, but her mom is the one who vacuums once in a while and changes the bed linen every Saturday morning (a chore she insists will be Gwendy's when she turns thirteen—some birthday present that will be). Mom mustn't find the box because moms want to know everything.

She next considers the attic, but what if her parents finally decide to clean it out and have a yard sale instead of just talking about it? The same is true of the storage space over the garage. Gwendy has a thought (novel now in its adult implications, later to become a tiresome truth): secrets are a problem, maybe the biggest problem of all. They weigh on the mind and take up space in the world.

Then she remembers the oak tree in the back yard, with the tire swing she hardly ever uses anymore—twelve is too old for such baby amusements. There's a shallow cavern beneath the tree's gnarl of roots. She used to curl up in there sometimes during games of hide-and-seek with her friends. She's too big for it now (*I'm thinking you might top out around five-ten or -eleven before you're done,* Mr. Farris told her), but it's a natural for the box, and the canvas bag will keep it dry if it rains. If it really *pours,* she'll have to come out and rescue it.

She tucks it away there, starts back to the house, then remembers the silver dollar. She returns to the tree and slips it into the bag with the box.

Gwendy thinks that her parents will see something strange has happened to her when they come home, that she's different, but they don't. They are wrapped up in their own affairs, as usual—Dad at the insurance office, Mom at Castle Rock Ford, where she's a secretary—and of course they have a few drinks. They always do. Gwendy has one helping of everything at dinner, and cleans her plate, but refuses a slice of the chocolate cake Dad brought home from the Castle Rock Bake Shop, next door to where he works.

"Oh my God, are you sick?" Dad asks.

Gwendy smiles. "Probably."

She's sure she'll lie awake until late, thinking about her encounter with Mr. Farris and the button box hidden under the backyard oak, but she doesn't. She thinks, *Light green for Asia, dark green for Africa, yellow for Australia...*and that's where she falls asleep until the next morning, when it's time to eat a big bowl of cereal with fruit, and then charge up the Suicide Stairs once more.

When she comes back, muscles glowing and stomach growling, she retrieves the canvas bag from under the tree, takes out the box, and uses her pinky to pull the lever on the left, near the red button (*whatever you want*, Mr. Farris said when she asked about that one). The slot opens and the shelf slides out. On it is a chocolate turtle, small but perfect, the shell a marvel of engraved plating. She tosses the turtle into her mouth. The sweetness blooms. Her hunger disappears, although when lunchtime comes, she will eat all of the bologna-and-cheese sandwich her mother has left her, plus some salad with French dressing, and a big glass of milk. She glances at the leftover cake in its plastic container. It looks good, but that's just an intellectual

29

appreciation. She would feel the same way about a cool two-page spread in a *Dr. Strange* comic book, but she wouldn't want to eat it, and she doesn't want to eat any cake, either.

That afternoon she goes bike-riding with her friend Olive, and then they spend the rest of the afternoon in Olive's bedroom, listening to records and talking about the upcoming school year. The prospect of going to Castle Rock Middle fills them with dread and excitement.

Back home, before her parents arrive, Gwendy takes the button box out of its hiding place again and pulls what she'll come to think of as the Money Lever. Nothing happens; the slot doesn't even open. Well, that's all right. Perhaps because she is an only child with no competition, Gwendy isn't greedy. When the little chocolates run out, she'll miss them more than any silver dollars. She hopes that won't happen for a while, but when it does, okay. *C'est la vie*, as her dad likes to say. Or *merde se*, which means shit happens.

Before returning the box, she looks at the buttons and names the continents they stand for. She touches them one by one. They draw her; she likes the way each touch seems to fill her with a different color, but she steers clear of the black one. That one is scary.

Well...they're all a little scary, but the black one is like a large dark mole, disfiguring and perhaps cancerous.

On Saturday, the Petersons pile into the Subaru station wagon and go to visit Dad's sister in Yarmouth. Gwendy usually enjoys these visits, because Aunt Dottie and Uncle Jim's twin girls are almost exactly her age, and the three of them always have fun together. There's usually a movie-show on Saturday night (this time a double feature at the Pride's Corner Drive-In, *Thunderbolt and Lightfoot*, plus *Gone in 60 Seconds*), and the girls lie out on the ground in sleeping bags, chattering away when the movie gets boring.

Gwendy has fun this time, too, but her thoughts keep turning to the button box. What if someone should find it and steal it? She knows that's unlikely—a burglar would just stick to the house, and not go searching under backyard trees—but the thought preys on her mind. Part of this is possessiveness; it's *hers*. Part of it is wishing for the little chocolate treats. Most of it, however, has to do with the buttons. A thief would see them, wonder what they were for, and push them. What would happen then? Especially if he pushed the black one? She's already starting to think of it as the Cancer Button.

When her mother says she wants to leave early on Sunday (there's going to be a Ladies Aid meeting, and Mrs. Peterson is treasurer this year), Gwendy is relieved. When they get home, she changes into her old jeans and goes out back. She swings in the tire for a little while, then pretends to drop something and goes to one knee, as if to look for it. What she's really looking for is the canvas bag. It's right where it belongs...but that is not enough. Furtively, she reaches between two of the gnarled roots and feels the box inside. One of the buttons is right under her first two fingers—she can feel its convex shape—and she withdraws her hand fast, as if she had touched a hot stove burner. Still, she is relieved. At least until a shadow falls over her.

"Want me to give you a swing, sweetie?" her dad asks.

"No," she says, getting up and brushing her knees. "I'm really too big for it now. Guess I'll go inside and watch TV."

He gives her a hug, pushes her glasses up on her nose, then strokes his fingers through her blonde hair, loosening a few tangles. "You're getting so tall," he says. "But you'll always be my little girl. Right, Gwennie?"

"You got it, Daddy-O," she says, and heads back inside. Before turning on the TV, she looks out into the yard from the window over the sink (no longer having to stand on tip-toe to do it). She watches her

father give the tire swing a push. She waits to see
if he will drop to his knees, perhaps curious about
what she was looking for. Or at. When he turns and
heads for the garage instead, Gwendy goes into the
living room, turns on *Soul Train*, and dances along
with Marvin Gaye.

3

WHEN SHE COMES BACK from her run up the Suicide Stairs on Monday, the lever by the red button dispenses a small chocolate kitty. She tries the other lever, not really expecting anything, but the slot opens, the shelf comes out, and on it is another 1891 silver dollar with nary a mark or a scratch on either side, the kind of coin she will come to know as uncirculated. Gwendy huffs on it, misting the features of Anna Willess Williams, then rubs the long-gone Philadelphia matron bright again on her shirt. Now she has two silver dollars, and if Mr. Farris was right about their worth, it's almost enough money for a year's tuition at the University of Maine. Good thing college is years away, because how could a twelve-year-old kid sell such valuable coins? Think of the questions they would raise!

Think of the questions the box would raise!

She touches the buttons again, one by one, avoiding the horrid black one but this time lingering on the red one, the tip of her finger circling around and around, feeling the oddest combination of distress and sensuous pleasure. At last she slides the button box back into its bag, stashes it, and bikes to Olive's house. They make strawberry turnovers under the watchful eye of Olive's mom, then go upstairs and put on Olive's records again. The door opens and Olive's mom comes in, but not to tell them they must lower the volume, as both girls expected. No, she wants to dance, too. It's fun. The three of them dance around and laugh like crazy, and when Gwendy goes home, she eats a big meal.

No seconds, though.

4

CASTLE ROCK MIDDLE TURNS out to be okay. Gwendy reconnects with her old friends and makes some new ones. She notices some of the boys eyeing her, which is okay because none of them is Frankie Stone and none of them call her Goodyear. Thanks to the Suicide Stairs, that nickname has been laid to rest. For her birthday in October, she gets a poster of Robby Benson, a little TV for her room (oh God, the joy) and lessons on how to change her own bed (not joyful but not bad). She makes the soccer team and the girls' track team, where she quickly becomes a standout.

The chocolate treats continue to come, no two ever the same, the detail always amazing. Every week or two there's also a silver dollar, always dated 1891. Her fingers linger longer and longer on the red button, and sometimes she hears herself whispering, "Whatever you want, whatever you want."

Miss Chiles, Gwendy's seventh grade history teacher, is young and pretty and dedicated to making her classes as interesting as possible. Sometimes her efforts are lame, but every once in a while they succeed splendidly. Just before the Christmas vacation, she announces that their first class in the new year will be Curiosity Day. Each pupil is to think of one historical thing they wonder about, and Miss Chiles will try to satisfy their curiosity. If she cannot, she'll throw the question to the class, for discussion and speculation.

"Just no questions about the sex lives of the presidents," she says, which makes the boys roar with laughter and the girls giggle hysterically.

When the day comes, the questions cover a wide range. Frankie Stone wants to know if the Aztecs really ate human hearts, and Billy Day wants to know who made the statues on Easter Island, but most of the questions on Curiosity Day in January of 1975 are what-ifs. What if the South had won the Civil War? What if George Washington had died of, like, starvation or frostbite at Valley Forge? What if Hitler had drowned in the bathtub when he was a baby?

When Gwendy's turn comes, she is prepared, but still a tiny bit nervous. "I don't know if this actually fits the assignment or not," she says, "but I think it might at least have historical…um…"

"Historical implications?" Miss Chiles asks.

"Yes! That!"

"Fine. Lay it on us."

"What if you had a button, a special magic button, and if you pushed it, you could kill somebody, or maybe just make them disappear, or blow up any place you were thinking of? What person would you make disappear, or what place would you blow up?"

A respectful silence falls as the class considers this wonderfully bloodthirsty concept, but Miss Chiles is frowning. "As a rule," she says, "erasing people from the world, either by murder or disappearance, is a very bad idea. So is blowing up *any* place."

Nancy Riordan says, "What about Hiroshima and Nagasaki? Are you saying blowing them up was bad?"

Miss Chiles looks taken aback. "No, not exactly," she says, "but think of all the innocent civilians that were killed when we bombed those cities. The women and children. The babies. And the radiation afterward! That killed even more."

"I get that," Joey Lawrence says, "but my grampa fought the Japs in the war, he was on Guadalcanal and Tarawa, and he said lots of the guys he fought with died. He said it was a miracle *he* didn't die. Grampy says dropping those bombs kept us from having to invade Japan, and we might have lost a million men if we had to do that."

The idea of killing someone (or making them disappear) has kind of gotten lost, but that's okay with Gwendy. She's listening, rapt.

"That's a very good point," Miss Chiles says. "Class, what do you think? Would you destroy a place if you could, in spite of the loss of civilian life? And if so, which place, and why?"

They talk about it for the rest of the class. Hanoi, says Henry Dussault. Knock out that guy Ho Chi Minh and end the stupid Vietnam War once and for all. Many agree with this. Ginny Brooks thinks it would be just grand if Russia could be obliterated. Mindy Ellerton is for eradicating China, because her dad says the Chinese are willing to start a nuclear war because they have so many people. Frankie Stone suggests getting rid of the American ghettos, where "those black people are making dope and killing cops."

After school, while Gwendy is getting her Huffy out of the bike rack, Miss Chiles comes over to her, smiling. "I just wanted to thank you for your question," she says. "I was a little shocked by it to begin with, but that turned out to be one of the best classes we've had this year. I believe everybody participated but you, which is strange, since you posed the question in the first place. Is there a place you would blow up, if you had that power? Or someone you'd…er…get rid of?"

Gwendy smiles back. "I don't know," she says. "That's why I asked the question."

"Good thing there isn't really a button like that," Miss Chiles says.

"But there is," Gwendy says. "Nixon has one. So does Brezhnev. Some other people, too."

Having given Miss Chiles this lesson—not in history, but in current events—Gwendy rides away on a bike that is rapidly becoming too small for her.

5

In June of 1975, Gwendy stops wearing her glasses.

Mrs. Peterson remonstrates with her. "I know that girls your age start thinking about boys, I haven't forgotten everything about being thirteen, but that saying about how boys don't make passes at girls who wear glasses is just—don't tell your father I said this—full of shit. The truth, Gwennie, is that boys will make passes at anything in a skirt, and you're far too young for that business, anyway."

"Mom, how old were you when you first made out with a boy?"

"Sixteen," says Mrs. Peterson without hesitation. She was actually eleven, kissing with Georgie McClelland, up in the loft of the McClelland barn. Oh, they smacked up a storm. "And listen, Gwennie, you're a very pretty girl, with or without glasses."

43

"It's nice of you to say so," Gwendy tells her, "but I really see better without them. They hurt my eyes now."

Mrs. Peterson doesn't believe it, so she takes her daughter to Dr. Emerson, the Rock's resident optician. He doesn't believe it, either...at least until Gwendy hands him her glasses and then reads the eye chart all the way to the bottom.

"Well I'll be darned," he says. "I've heard of this, but it's extremely rare. You must have been eating a lot of carrots, Gwendy."

"I guess that must be it," she smiles, thinking, *It's chocolates I've been eating. Magic chocolate animals, and they never run out.*

6

GWENDY'S WORRIES ABOUT THE box being discovered
or stolen are like a constant background hum in her
head, but those worries never come close to ruling her
life. It occurs to her that might have been one of the
reasons why Mr. Farris gave it to her. Why he said *you
are the one.*

She does well in her classes, she has a big role in
the eighth grade play (and never forgets a single line),
she continues to run track. Track is the best; when
that runner's high kicks in, even the background hum
of worry disappears. Sometimes she resents Mr. Farris
for saddling her with the responsibility of the box,
but mostly she doesn't. As he told her, it gives gifts.
Small recompense, he said, but the gifts don't seem so
small to Gwendy; her memory is better, she no longer

wants to eat everything in the fridge, her vision is twenty-twenty, she can run like the wind, and there's something else, too. Her mother called her very pretty, but her friend Olive is willing to go farther.

"Jesus, you're gorgeous," she says to Gwendy one day, not sounding pleased about it. They are in Olive's room again, this time discussing the mysteries of high school, which they will soon begin to unravel. "No more glasses, and not even one frickin' pimple. It's not fair. You'll have to beat the guys off with a stick."

Gwendy laughs it off, but she knows that Olive is onto something. She really *is* good-looking, and gorgeosity isn't out of the realm of possibility at some point in the future. Perhaps by the time she gets to college. Only when she goes away to school, what will she do with the button box? She can't simply leave it under the tree in the backyard, can she?

Henry Dussault asks her to the freshman mixer dance on their first Friday night of high school, holds her hand on the walk home, and kisses her when they get to the Peterson house. It's not bad, being kissed, except Henry's breath is sort of yuck. She hopes the next boy with whom she lip-locks will be a regular Listerine user.

She wakes up at two o'clock on the morning after the dance, with her hands pressed over her mouth to hold in a scream, still in the grip of the most vivid nightmare she's ever had. In it, she looked out the window over the kitchen sink and saw Henry sitting in the tire swing (which Gwendy's dad actually took down a year ago). He had the button box in his lap. Gwendy rushed out, shouting at him, telling him not to press any of the buttons, especially not the black one.

Oh, you mean this one? Henry asked, grinning, and jammed his thumb down on the Cancer Button.

Above them, the sky went dark. The ground began to rumble like a live thing. Gwendy knew that all over the world, famous landmarks were falling and seas were rising. In moments—*mere moments*—the planet was going to explode like an apple with a firecracker stuffed in it, and between Mars and Venus there would be nothing but a second asteroid belt.

"A dream," Gwendy says, going to her bedroom window. "A dream, a dream, nothing but a dream."

Yes. The tree is there, now minus the tire swing, and there's no Henry Dussault in sight. But if he had the box, and knew what each button stood for, what would he do? Push the red one and blow up Hanoi? Or say the hell with it and push the light green one?

"And blow up all of Asia," she whispers. Because yes, that's what the buttons do. She knew from the first, just as Mr. Farris said. The violet one blows up South America, the orange one blows up Europe, the red one does whatever you want, whatever you're thinking of. And the black one?

The black one blows up everything.

"That can't be," she whispers to herself as she goes back to bed. "It's insane."

Only the world is insane. You only have to watch the news to know it.

When she comes home from school the next day, Gwendy goes down to the basement with a hammer and a chisel. The walls are stone, and she is able to pry one out in the farthest corner. She uses the chisel to deepen this hidey-hole until it's big enough for the button box. She checks her watch constantly as she works, knowing her father will be home at five, her mother by five-thirty at the latest.

She runs to the tree, gets the canvas bag with the button box and her silver dollars inside (the silver dollars are now much heavier than the box, although they *came* from the box), and runs back to the house. The hole is just big enough. And the stone fits into place like the last piece of a puzzle. For good measure, she drags an old bureau in front of it, and at last feels at peace. Henry won't be able to find it now. *Nobody* will be able to find it.

"I ought to throw the goddamned thing in Castle Lake," she whispers as she climbs the cellar stairs. "Be done with it." Only she knows she could never do that. It's hers, at least unless Mr. Farris comes back to claim it. Sometimes she hopes he will. Sometimes she hopes he never will.

When Mr. Peterson comes home, he looks at Gwendy with some concern. "You're all sweaty," he says. "Do you feel all right?"

She smiles. "Been running, that's all. I'm fine."

And mostly, she is.

7

BY THE SUMMER AFTER her freshman year, Gwendy is feeling *very* fine, indeed.

For starters, she's grown another inch since school let out and, even though it's not yet the Fourth of July, she's sporting a killer suntan. Unlike most of her classmates, Gwendy has never had much of a suntan before. In fact, the previous summer was the first summer of her life that she'd dared to wear a swimsuit in public, and even then, she'd settled on a modest one-piece. A granny suit, her best friend Olive had teased one afternoon at the community swimming pool.

But that was then and this is now; no more granny suits this summer. In early June, Mrs. Peterson and Gwendy drive to the mall in downtown Castle Rock and come home with matching flip-flops and a pair of colorful bikinis. Bright yellow and even brighter red with little white polka dots. The yellow bathing suit quickly becomes Gwendy's favorite. She will never admit it to anyone else, but when Gwendy studies herself in the full-length mirror in the privacy of her bedroom, she secretly believes she resembles the girl from the Coppertone ad. This never fails to please her.

But it's more than just bronzed legs and teeny-weenie polka dot bikinis. Other things are better, too. Take her parents, for instance. She would've never gone so far as to label mom and dad as alcoholics—not quite, and never out loud to anyone—but she knows they used to drink too much, and she thinks she knows the reason for this: somewhere along the way, say about the time Gwendy was finishing up the third grade, her parents had fallen out of love with each other. Just like in the movies. Nightly martinis and the business section of the newspaper (for Mr. Peterson) and sloe gin fizzes and romance novels (for Mrs. Peterson) had gradually replaced after-dinner family walks around the neighborhood and jigsaw puzzles at the dining room table.

For the better part of her elementary school years, Gwendy suffered this familial deterioration with a sense of silent worry. No one said a word to her about what was going on, and she didn't say a word to anyone else either, especially not her mother or father. She wouldn't even have known how to begin such a conversation.

Then, not long after the arrival of the button box, everything began to change.

Mr. Peterson showed up early from work one evening with a bouquet of daisies (Mrs. Peterson's favorites) and news of an unexpected promotion at the insurance office. They celebrated this good fortune with a pizza dinner and ice cream sundaes and—surprise—a long walk around the neighborhood.

Then, sometime early last winter, Gwendy noticed that the drinking had stopped. Not slowed down, but completely stopped. One day after school, before her parents got home from work, she searched the house from top to bottom, and didn't find a single bottle of booze anywhere. Even the old fridge out in the garage was empty of Mr. Peterson's favorite beer, Black Label. It had been replaced by a case of Dad's Root Beer.

That night, while her father was getting spaghetti from Gino's, Gwendy asked her mother if they had really quit drinking. Mrs. Peterson laughed. "If you mean did we join AA or stand in front of Father O'Malley and take the pledge, we didn't."

"Well…whose idea was it? Yours or his?"

Gwendy's mother looked vague. "I don't think we even discussed it."

Gwendy left it there. Another of her father's sayings seemed applicable: *Don't look a gift horse in the mouth.*

And just a week later, the cherry on top of this minor miracle: Gwendy walked out into the back yard to ask her father for a ride to the library and was startled to find Mr. and Mrs. Peterson holding hands and smiling at each other. Just standing there in their winter coats with their breath frosting the air, looking into each other's eyes like reunited lovers of *Days of Our Lives*. Gwendy, mouth gaping open, stopped in her tracks and took in this tableau. Tears prickled her eyes. She hadn't seen them looking at each other that way in she couldn't remember how long. Maybe never. Stopped dead in her tracks at the foot of the kitchen stoop, her earmuffs dangling from one mittened hand, she thought of Mr. Farris and his magic box.

It did this. I don't know how or why, but it did this. It's not just me. It's like a kind of…I don't know…

"An umbrella," she whispered, and that was just right. An umbrella that could shade her family from too much sun and also keep the rain off. Everything was okay, and as long as a strong wind didn't come up and blow the umbrella inside out, things would stay okay. And why would that happen? *It won't. It can't. Not as long as I take care of the box. I have to. It's my button box now.*

8

ON A THURSDAY NIGHT in early August, Gwendy is hauling a garbage can to the bottom of the driveway when Frankie Stone swings to the curb in front of her in his blue El Camino. The Rolling Stones are blaring from the car stereo and Gwendy catches a whiff of marijuana wafting from the open window. He turns down the music. "Wanna go for a ride, sexy?"

Frankie Stone has grown up, but not in a good way. He sports greasy brown hair, a shotgun pattern of acne scattered across his face, and a homemade AC/DC tattoo on one arm. He also suffers from the worst case of body odor Gwendy has ever come across. There are whispers that he fed a hippie girl roofies at a concert and then raped her. Probably not true, she knows about the vicious rumors kids start, but he sure *looks* like someone who'd slip roofies into a girl's wine cooler.

"I can't," Gwendy says, wishing she were wearing more than just cut-off jean shorts and a tank top. "I have to do my homework."

"Homework?" Frankie scowls. "C'mon, who the fuck does homework in the summer?"

"It's…I'm taking a summer class at the community college."

Frankie leans out the window, and even though he's still a good ten feet away from her, Gwendy can smell his breath. "You wouldn't be lying to me now, would you, pretty girl?" He grins.

"I'm not lying. Have a good night, Frankie. I better get inside and hit the books."

Gwendy turns and starts walking up the driveway, feeling good about the way she handled him. She hasn't taken but four or five steps when something hard plunks her in the back of her neck. She cries out, not hurt but surprised, and turns back to the street. A beer can spins lazily at her feet, spitting foam onto the pavement.

"Just like the rest of the stuck up bitches," Frankie says. "I thought you were different, but you're not. Think you're too good for everyone."

Gwendy reaches up and rubs the back of her neck. A nasty bump has already risen there, and she flinches when her fingers touch it. "You need to go, Frankie. Before I get my father."

"Fuck your father, and fuck you, too. I knew you when you were nothin but an ugly fuckin chubber." Frankie points a finger-gun at her and smiles. "It'll come back, too. Fat girls turn into fat women. It never fails. See you around, Goodyear."

Then he's gone, middle finger jutting out the window, tires burning rubber. Only now does Gwendy allow the tears to come as she runs inside the house.

That night she dreams about Frankie Stone. In the dream, she doesn't stand there helpless in the driveway with her heart in her throat. In the dream, she rushes at Frankie, and before he can peel out, she lunges through the open driver's window and grabs his left arm. She twists until she hears—and feels—the bones snapping beneath her hands. And as he screams, she says, *How's that boner now, Frankie Stoner? More like two inches than two feet, I bet. You never should have fucked with the Queen of the Button Box.*

She wakes up in the morning and remembers the dream with a sleepy smile, but as with most dreams, it vanishes with the rising sun. She doesn't think of it again until two weeks later, during a breakfast conversation with her father on a lazy Saturday morning. Mr. Peterson finishes his coffee and puts

61

down the newspaper. "Your pal Frankie Stone made the news."

Gwendy stops in mid-chew. "He's no pal of mine, I hate the guy. Why's he in the paper?"

"Car accident last night out on Hanson Road. Probably drunk, although it doesn't say so. Hit a tree. He's okay, but pretty banged up."

"How banged up?"

"Bunch of stitches in his head and shoulder. Cuts all over his face. Broken arm. Multiple breaks, according to the story. Going to take a long time to heal. Want to see for yourself?"

He pushes the paper across the table. Gwendy pushes it back, then carefully puts down her fork. She knows she won't be able to eat another bite, just as she knows without asking that the broken arm Frankie Stone suffered is his left one.

That night, in bed, trying to sweep away the troubled thoughts swirling inside her head, Gwendy counts how many days of summer vacation remain before she has to return to school.

This is August 22nd, 1977. Exactly three years to the day from when Mr. Farris and the button box came into her life.

9

A WEEK BEFORE GWENDY starts the tenth grade at Castle Rock High, she runs the Suicide Stairs for the first time in almost a year. The day is mild and breezy, and she reaches the top without breaking much of a sweat. She stretches for a brief moment and glances down the length of her body: she can see her entire damn sneakers.

She walks to the railing and takes in the view. It's the kind of morning that makes you wish death didn't exist. She scans Dark Score Lake, then turns to the playground, empty now except for a young mother pushing a toddler on the baby swing. Her eyes finally settle on the bench where she met Mr. Farris. She walks over to it and sits down.

More and more often lately, a little voice inside her head is asking questions she doesn't have answers for.

Why you, Gwendy Peterson? Out of all the people in this round world, why did he choose you?

And there are other, scarier, questions, too: *Where did he come from? Why was he keeping an eye on me? (*His exact words!*) What the hell* is *that box...and what is it doing to me?*

Gwendy sits on the bench for a long time, thinking and watching the clouds drift past. After a while, she gets up and jogs down the Suicide Stairs and home again. The questions remain: *How much of her life is her own doing, and how much the doing of the box with its treats and buttons?*

10

SOPHOMORE YEAR OPENS WITH a bang. Within a month of the first day of classes, Gwendy is elected Class President, named captain of the junior varsity soccer team, and asked to the homecoming dance by Harold Perkins, a handsome senior on the football squad (alas, the homecoming date never happens, as Gwendy dumps poor Harold after he repeatedly tries to feel her up at a drive-in showing of *Damnation Alley* on their first date). Plenty of time for touchie-feelie later, as her mother likes to say.

For her sixteenth birthday in October, she gets a poster of the Eagles standing in front of Hotel California (*"You can check out any time you like, but you can never leave"*), a new stereo with both eight track and cassette decks, and a promise from her father to teach her how to drive now that she's of legal age.

The chocolate treats continue to come, no two ever the same, the detail always amazing. The tiny slice of heaven Gwendy devoured just this morning before school was a giraffe, and she purposely skipped brushing her teeth afterward. She wanted to savor the remarkable taste for as long as she could.

Gwendy doesn't pull the other small lever nearly as often as she once did, for no other reason than she's finally run out of space to hide the silver coins. For now, the chocolate is enough.

She still thinks about Mr. Farris, not quite as often and usually in the long, empty hours of the night when she tries to remember exactly what he looked like or how his voice sounded. She's almost sure she once saw him in the crowd at the Castle Rock Halloween Fair, but she was high atop the Ferris wheel at that moment, and by the time the ride ended, he was gone, swallowed by the hordes of people flocking down the midway. Another time she went into a Portland coin shop with one of the silver dollars. The worth had gone up; the man offered her $750 for one of her 1891 Morgans, saying he'd never seen a better one. Gwendy refused, telling him (on the spur of the moment) that it was a gift from her grandfather and she only wanted to know what it was worth. Leaving, she saw a man looking at her from across the street, a man wearing a neat little black hat. Farris—if it *was* Farris—gave her a fleeting smile, and disappeared around the corner.

Watching her? Keeping track? Is it possible? She thinks it is.

And she still thinks about the buttons, of course, especially the red one. She sometimes finds herself sitting cross-legged on the cold basement floor, holding the button box in her lap, staring at that red button in a kind of daze and caressing it with the tip of her finger. She wonders what would happen if she pushed the red button without a clear choice of a place to blow up. What then? Who would decide what was destroyed? God? The box?

A few weeks after her trip to the coin shop, Gwendy decides it's time to find out about the red button once and for all.

Instead of spending her fifth period study hall in the library, she heads for Mr. Anderson's empty World History classroom. There's a reason for this: the pair of pull-down maps that are attached to Mr. Anderson's chalkboard.

Gwendy has considered a number of possible targets for the red button. She hates that word—*target*—but it fits, and she can't think of anything better. Among her initial options: the Castle Rock dump, a stretch of trashy, pulped-over woods beyond the railroad tracks, and the old abandoned Phillips 66 gas station where kids hang out and smoke dope.

In the end, she decides to not only target someplace outside of Castle Rock, but also the entire country. Better safe than sorry.

She walks behind Mr. Anderson's desk and carefully studies the map, focusing first on Australia (where, she recently learned, over one-third of the country is desert) before moving on to Africa (those poor folks have enough problems) and finally settling on South America.

From her history notes, Gwendy remembers two important facts that aid this decision: South America harbors thirty-five of the fifty least-developed countries in the world, and a similar percentage of the least-populated countries in the world.

Now that the choice has been made, Gwendy doesn't waste any time. She scribbles down the names of three small countries in her spiral notebook, one from the north, one from the middle of the continent, and one from the south. Then, she hurries to the library to do more research. She looks at pictures and makes a list of the most godforsaken ones.

Later that afternoon, Gwendy sits down in front of her bedroom closet and balances the button box on her lap.

She places a shaky finger on top of the red button.

She closes her eyes and pictures one tiny part of a faraway country. Dense, tangled vegetation. An expanse of wild jungle where no people live. As many details as she can manage.

She holds the image in her head and pushes the red button.

Nothing happens. It doesn't go down.

Gwendy stabs at the red button a second and third time. It doesn't budge under her finger. The part about the buttons was a practical joke, it seems. And gullible Gwendy Peterson believed it.

Almost relieved, she starts to return the button box to the closet when Mr. Farris's words suddenly come back to her: *The buttons are very hard to push. You have to use your thumb, and put some real muscle into it. Which is a good thing, believe me.*

She lowers the box to her lap again—and uses her thumb to press the red button. She puts all her weight on it. This time, there's a barely audible *click,* and Gwendy feels the button depress.

She stares at the box for a moment, thinking *Some trees and maybe a few animals. A small earthquake or maybe a fire. Surely no more than that.* Then she returns it to its hiding place in the wall of the basement. Her face feels warm and her stomach hurts. Does that mean it's working?

11

GWENDY WAKES UP THE next morning running a fever. She stays home from school and spends most of the day sleeping. She emerges from her bedroom later that evening, feeling as good as new, and discovers her parents watching the news in silence. She can tell from the expressions on their faces that something is wrong. She eases down on the sofa next to her mother and watches in horror as Charles Gibson takes them to Guyana—a faraway country of which she recently learned a few salient details. There a cult leader by the name of Jim Jones has committed suicide and ordered over nine hundred of his followers to do the same.

Grainy photographs flash on the television screen. Bodies laid out in rows, thick jungle looming in the background. Couples in a lovers' embrace. Mothers clutching babies to still chests. So many children. Faces distorted in agony. Flies crawling all over everything. According to Charles Gibson, nurses squirted the poison down the kiddies' throats before taking their own doses.

Gwendy returns to her bedroom without comment and slips on tennis shoes and a sweatshirt. She thinks about running Suicide Stairs but decides against it, vaguely afraid of an impulse to throw herself off. Instead, she travels a three-mile loop around the neighborhood, her footsteps slapping a staccato rhythm on the cold pavement, crisp autumn air blushing her cheeks. *I did that*, she thinks, picturing flies swarming over dead babies. *I didn't mean to, but I did.*

12

"You LOOKED RIGHT AT me," Olive says. Her voice is calm, but her eyes are burning. "I don't know how you can say you didn't see me standing there."

"I didn't. I swear."

They are sitting in Gwendy's bedroom after school, listening to the new Billy Joel album and supposedly studying for an English mid-term. Now it's obvious Olive came over with what she likes to call ISSUES. Olive often has ISSUES these days.

"I find that hard to believe."

Gwendy's eyes go wide. "You're calling me a liar? Why in the world would I walk right by you without saying hello?"

Olive shrugs, her lips pressed tight. "Maybe you didn't want all your cool friends to know you used to hang out with other lowly sophomores."

"That's stupid. You're my best friend, Olive. Everyone knows that."

Olive barks out a laugh. "Best friend? Do you know the last time we've done something on a weekend? Forget Friday and Saturday nights with all your dates and parties and bonfires. I'm talking the entire weekend, any time at all."

"I've been really busy," Gwendy says, looking away. She knows her friend is right, but why does she have to be so sensitive? "I'm sorry."

"And you don't even like half those guys. Bobby Crawford asks you out and you giggle and twirl your hair and say 'Sure, why not?' even though you barely know his name and could care less about him."

And, just like that, Gwendy understands. *How could I be so stupid?* she wonders. "I didn't know you liked Bobby." She scoots across the bedroom floor and puts her hand on her friend's knee. "I swear I didn't. I'm sorry."

Olive doesn't say anything. Apparently the ISSUE remains.

"That was months ago. Bobby's a really nice guy, but that's the only time I went out with him. If you want, I can call him and tell him about you—"

Olive pushes Gwendy's hand away and gets to her feet. "I don't need your goddamn charity." She bends down and gathers her books and folders into her arms.

"It's not charity. I just thought—"

"That's your problem," Olive says, pulling away again. "You only think about yourself. You're selfish." She stomps out of the bedroom and slams the door behind her.

Gwendy stands there in disbelief, her body trembling with hurt. Then the hurt blooms into anger. "Go to hell!" she screams at the closed door. "If you want to address an issue, try your *jealous bone*!"

She flings herself back on the bed, tears streaming down her face, the hurtful words echoing: *You only think about yourself. You're selfish.*

"That's not true," Gwendy whispers to the empty room. "I think about others. I try to be a good person. I made a mistake about Guyana, but I was…I was tricked into it, and I wasn't the one who poisoned them. *It wasn't me.*" Except it sort of was.

Gwendy cries herself to sleep and dreams of nurses bearing syringes of Kool-Aid death to small children.

13

SHE TRIES TO SMOOTH things over the next day at school, but Olive refuses to talk to her. The following day, Friday, is more of the same. Just before the final bell rings, Gwendy slips a handwritten apology note inside Olive's locker and hopes for the best.

On Saturday night, Gwendy and her date, a junior named Walter Dean, stop by the arcade on their way to an early movie. During the car ride over, Walter pulls out a bottle of wine he lifted from his mother's stash, and although Gwendy usually passes on such offers, tonight she helps herself. She's sad and confused and hopes the buzz will help.

It doesn't. It only gives her a mild headache.

Gwendy nods hello to several classmates as they enter the arcade and is surprised to see Olive standing in line at the snack bar. Hopeful, she flips her a tentative wave, but once again Olive ignores her. A moment later, Olive walks right past her, large soda cradled in her arms, nose in the air, giggling with a pack of girls Gwendy recognizes from a neighboring high school.

"What's her problem?" Walter asks, before sliding a quarter into a Space Invaders machine.

"Long story." Gwendy stares after her friend and her anger returns. She feels her face flush with annoyance. *She knows what it was like for me. Hey, Goodyear, where's the football game? Hey, Goodyear, how's the view up there? She should be happy for me. She should be—*

Twenty feet away from her, Olive screams as someone bumps her arm, sending a cascade of ice-cold soda all over her face and down the front of her brand new sweater. Kids point and start to laugh. Olive looks around in embarrassment, her eyes finally settling on Gwendy, and then she storms away and disappears into the public restroom.

Gwendy, remembering her dream about Frankie Stone, suddenly wants to go home and shut the door of her room and crawl under the covers.

14

THE DAY BEFORE SHE'S scheduled to attend junior prom with Walter Dean, Gwendy rolls out of bed late to discover that the basement has flooded overnight after a particularly heavy spring thunderstorm.

"It's wetter than a taco fart down there and just as smelly," Mr. Peterson tells her. "You sure you want to go down?"

Gwendy nods, trying to hide her rising panic. "I need to check on some old books and a pile of clothes I left for the laundry."

Mr. Peterson shrugs his shoulders and returns his gaze to the small television on the kitchen counter. "Make sure you take off your shoes before you go. And hey, might want to wear a life preserver."

Gwendy hurries down the basement stairs before he can change his mind and wades into a pool of ankle-high scummy gray water. Earlier this morning Mr. Peterson managed to unclog the sump pump, and Gwendy can hear it chugging away over in the far corner, but it's going to have a long day. She can tell by the water line that marks the basement's stone walls that the floodwater has dropped maybe two inches at the most.

She wades to the opposite side of the basement where the button box is hidden and pushes aside the old bureau. She drops to a knee in the corner and reaches down into the cloudy water, unable to see her hands, and works the stone free.

Her fingers touch wet canvas. She pulls the water-logged bag out of its hidey-hole, puts it aside, then picks up the loose stone and places it back into the wall so her father won't notice it once the water has finished receding.

She reaches to the side again for the canvas bag containing the box and coins—and it isn't there.

She flails her hands under the water, trying desperately to locate the bag, but it's nowhere to be found. Black dots swim in her vision and she suddenly feels light-headed. She realizes she's forgotten to breathe, so she opens her mouth and takes in a big gulp of foul, moldy basement air. Her eyes and brain immediately begin to clear.

Gwendy takes one more calming breath and once again reaches down into the dirty water, this time trying her other side. Right away, her fingers brush the canvas bag. She gets to her feet and like a weightlifter performing a deadlift squat, she raises the heavy bag to her waist and waddles her way across the basement to the shelves next to the washer and dryer. She grabs a couple of dry towels from an upper shelf and does the best she can to wrap the canvas bag.

"You okay down there?" her father hollers from upstairs. She hears footsteps on the ceiling above her. "Need any help? Scuba tank and fins, maybe?"

"No, no," Gwendy says, hurrying to make sure the bag is fully concealed. Her heart is a triphammer in her chest. "I'll be up in a few."

"If you say so." She listens to her father's muffled footsteps again, but going away. Thank God.

She grabs the bag again and shuffles across the flooded basement as fast as her tired legs will carry her, grunting with the weight of the box and the silver coins.

Once she is safely inside her bedroom, she locks the door behind her and unwraps the canvas bag. The button box appears undamaged, but how would she really know? She pulls the lever on the left side of the box and after a breathless moment when she is absolutely convinced the box is broken after all, the little shelf slides open without a sound and on it is a chocolate monkey the size of a jelly bean. She quickly stuffs the chocolate into her mouth and that gorgeous flavor takes her away again. She closes her eyes while it melts on her tongue.

The bag is ripped in several places and will have to be replaced, but Gwendy isn't worried about that. She looks around her bedroom and settles on the bottom of her closet, where her shoeboxes are stacked in messy piles. Her parents never bother with her closet these days.

She removes an old pair of boots from their oversized cardboard box and tosses them to the opposite end of the closet. She carefully places the button box inside and adds the pile of silver coins. Once the lid is securely back on the shoebox, she slides it—it's too heavy to pick up now; the cardboard would surely tear—into the shadows at the very back of her closet. Once that's done, she stacks other shoeboxes on top and in front of it.

She gets to her feet, backs up, and surveys her work. Convinced that she's done a competent job, she picks up the soaked canvas bag and heads for the kitchen to throw it away and grab some cereal for breakfast.

She lazes around the house the rest of the day, watching television and skimming her history book.

Every thirty minutes or so—more than a dozen times in all—she gets up from the sofa, walks down the hallway, and peeks her head into her bedroom to make sure the box is still safe.

The next night is the prom, and she finds that she actually has to force herself to put on her pink gown and make-up and leave the house.

Is this my life now? she thinks as she enters the Castle Rock gym. *Is that box my life?*

15

SELLING THE SILVER COINS isn't back on Gwendy's radar until she sees the advertising flyer taped to the front window of the Castle Rock Diner. After that, it's pretty much all she can think about. There was that one trip to the coin shop, true, but it was mostly of an exploratory nature. Now, however, things have changed. Gwendy wants to attend an Ivy League university after she graduates from high school—and those places don't come cheap. She plans to apply for grants and scholarships, and with her grades she's sure she'll get something, but enough? Probably not. *Surely* not.

What *is* a sure thing are the 1891 Morgan silver dollars stacked inside a shoebox in the back of her closet. Over a hundred of them at last count.

Gwendy knows from leafing through back issues of *COINage* magazine at the drug store that the fair-trade price of the Morgans is not just holding steady; their value is still rising. According to the magazine, inflation and global unrest are driving the market in gold and silver coins. Her first idea was to sell enough of the coins (maybe in Portland, more likely in Boston) to pay for college and figure out how to explain the sudden windfall only when it becomes absolutely necessary. Maybe she'll say she found it. Hard to believe, but also hard to disprove. (The best-laid plans of sixteen-year-olds are rarely thought out.)

The Coin & Stamp Show flyer gives Gwendy another idea. A better idea.

The plan is to take two of the silver dollars, enough to test the waters, and bike down to the VFW first thing this weekend to see what she can get for them. If they actually sell, and for real money, then she'll know.

16

THE FIRST THING GWENDY notices when she walks into the VFW at ten-fifteen on Saturday morning is the sheer size of the place. It didn't look nearly as spacious from the outside. The dealer tables are arranged in a long, enclosed rectangle. The sellers, mostly men, stand on the inside of the rectangle. The customers, of whom there are already more than two or three dozen, circle the tables with wary eyes and nervous fingers. There doesn't seem to be a discernible pattern to the set-up—coin dealers here, stamp hucksters there—and more than a few of the merchants deal in both. A couple even have rare sports and tobacco cards fanned out across their tables. She is flabbergasted to see a signed Mickey Mantle card priced at $2,900, but in a way, relieved. It makes her silver dollars look like pretty small beans in comparison.

She stands in the entryway and takes it all in. It's a whole new world, exotic and intimidating, and she feels overwhelmed. It must be obvious to anyone watching her because a nearby dealer calls out, "Ya lost, honey? Anything I can help ya with?"

He's a chubby man in his thirties wearing glasses and an Orioles baseball cap. There's food in his beard and a twinkle in his eyes.

Gwendy approaches his table. "I'm just looking right now, thanks."

"Looking to buy or looking to sell?" The man's eyes drop to Gwendy's bare legs and linger there longer than they should. When he looks up again, he's grinning and Gwendy doesn't like that twinkle anymore.

"Just looking," she says, quickly walking away.

She watches a man two tables down examining a tiny stamp with a magnifying glass and tweezers. She overhears him say, "I can go seventy dollars and that's already twenty over my limit. My wife will kill me if I..." She doesn't stick around to see if he seals the deal.

At the far end of the rectangle, she comes to a table covered exclusively with coins. She spots a Morgan silver dollar in the center of the last row. She takes this as a good sign. The man behind the table is bald and old, how old she's not entirely sure, but at least old enough to be a grandfather. He smiles at Gwendy and doesn't glance at her legs, which is a good start. He taps the nametag attached to his shirt. "Name's Jon Leonard, like it says, but I go by Lenny to my friends. You look friendly, so is there anything special I can help you with today? Got a Lincoln penny book you want to finish filling out? Maybe looking for a buffalo nickel or a few commemorative state quarters? I got a Utah, very good condition and scarce."

"I actually have something I'd like to sell. Maybe."

"Uh-huh, okay, lemme take a look and I can tell you if we might do some business."

Gwendy takes the coins—each in its own little plastic envelope—out of her pocket and hands them to him. Lenny's fingers are thick and gnarled, but he slips the coins out with practiced ease, holding them by their thickness, not touching the heads and tails sides. Gwendy notices his eyes flash wider. He whistles. "Mind if I ask where you got these?"

Gwendy tells him what she told the coin dealer in Portland. "My grandfather passed away recently and left them to me."

The man looks genuinely pained. "I'm really sorry to hear that, honey."

"Thank you," she says, and puts her hand out. "I'm Gwendy Peterson."

The man gives it a firm shake. "Gwendy. I like that."

"Me too," Gwendy says and smiles. "Good thing, since I'm stuck with it."

The man turns on a small desk light and uses a magnifying glass to examine the silver dollars. "Never seen one in mint condition before, and here you got two of em." He looks up at her. "How old are you, Miss Gwendy, if you don't mind my asking?"

"Sixteen."

The man snaps his fingers and points at her. "Looking to buy a car, I bet."

She shakes her head. "One day, but I'm thinking of selling these to make some money for college. I want to go to an Ivy League school after I graduate."

The man nods his head with approval. "Good for you." He studies the coins again with the magnifying glass. "Be honest with me now, Miss Gwendy, your folks know you're selling these?"

"Yes, sir, they do. They're okay with it because it's for a good cause."

His gaze turns shrewd. "But they're not with you, I notice."

Gwendy might not have been ready for this at fourteen, but she's older now, and can hit the occasional adult curveball. "They both said I have to start fending for myself sometime, and this might be a good place to start. Also, I read the magazine you've got there." She points. "*COINage*?"

"Uh-huh, uh-huh." Lenny puts down the magnifying glass and gives her his full attention. "Well, Miss Gwendy Peterson, a Morgan silver dollar of this vintage and in Near Mint condition can sell for anywhere from seven hundred and twenty-five dollars to eight hundred. A Morgan in *this* condition…" He shakes his head. "I honestly don't know."

Gwendy didn't practice this part—how could she?—but she really likes the old man, so she wings it. "My mom works at a car dealership, and they have a saying about some of the cars: 'Priced to sell.' So… could you pay eight hundred each? Would that be priced to sell?"

"Yes, ma'am, it would," he says with no hesitation. "Only are you sure? One of the bigger shops might be able to—"

"I'm sure. If you can pay eight hundred apiece, we have a deal."

The old man chuckles and sticks his hand out. "Then, Miss Gwendy Peterson, we have ourselves a deal." They shake on it. "I'll write you up a receipt and get you paid."

"Um…I'm sure you're trustworthy, Lenny, but I really wouldn't feel comfortable with a check."

"With me up in Toronto or down in D.C. tomorrow, who'd blame you?" He drops her a wink. "Besides, I got a saying of my own: Cash don't tattle. And what Uncle Sammy don't know about our business won't hurt him."

Lenny slips the coins into their transparent envelopes and disappears them somewhere beneath the table. Once he's counted out sixteen crisp one hundred dollar bills—Gwendy still can't believe this is happening—he writes a receipt, tears out a copy, and lays it atop the cash. "I put my phone number on there too in case your folks have any questions. How far is home?"

"About a mile. I rode my bike."

He considers that. "Lotta money for a young girl, Gwendy. Think maybe you should call your parents for a ride?"

"No need," she says, smiling. "I can take care of myself."

The old man's eyebrows dance as he laughs. "I bet you can."

He stuffs the money and the receipt into an envelope. He folds the envelope in half and uses about a yard of scotch tape to seal it tight. "See if that'll fit nice and snug in your shorts pocket," he says, handing over the envelope.

Gwendy stuffs it into her pocket and pats the outside. "Snug as a bug in a rug."

"I like you, girl, I do. Got style and got sand. A combination that can't be beat." Lenny turns to the dealer on his left. "Hank, you mind watching my table for a minute?"

"Only if you bring me back a soda," Hank says.

"Done." Lenny slips out from behind his table and escorts Gwendy to the door. "You sure you're going to be okay?"

"Positive. Thanks again, Mr. Lenny," she says, feeling the weight of the money inside her pocket. "I really appreciate it."

"The appreciation is all mine, Miss Gwendy." He holds the door open for her. "Good luck with the Ivy League."

17

GWENDY SQUINTS IN THE May sunlight as she unlocks her bike from a nearby tree. It never occurred to her this morning that the VFW wouldn't have a bike rack—then again, how many vets did you see cruising around Castle Rock on bicycles?

She pats her pocket to make sure the envelope is still nice and snug, then straddles her bike and pushes off. Halfway across the parking lot, she spots Frankie Stone and Jimmy Sines, checking car doors and peering into windows. Some unlucky person was going to walk out of the Coin & Stamp Show today and find their car ransacked.

Gwendy pedals faster, hoping to slip away unnoticed, but she's not that lucky.

"Hey, sugar tits!" Frankie yells from behind her, and then he's sprinting ahead and cutting her off, blocking her exit from the parking lot. He waves his arms at her. "Whoa, whoa, whoa!"

Gwendy skids to a stop in front him. "Leave me alone, Frankie."

It takes him a moment to catch his breath. "I just wanted to ask you a question, that's all."

"Then ask it and get out of my way." She glances around for an escape route.

Jimmy Sines emerges from behind a parked car. Stands on the other side of her with his arms crossed. He looks at Frankie. "Sugar tits, huh?"

Frankie grins. "This is the one I was telling you about." He walks closer to Gwendy, trails a finger up her leg. She swats it away.

"Ask your question and move."

"C'mon, don't be like that," he says. "I was just wondering how your ass is. You always had such a tight one. Must make it hard to take a shit." He's touching her leg again. Not just a finger; his whole hand.

"These boys bothering you, Miss Gwendy?"

All three of them turn and look. Lenny is standing there.

"Get lost, old man," Frankie says, taking a step toward him.

"I don't think so. You okay, Gwendy?"

"I'm okay now." She pushes off and starts pedaling. "Gotta get going or I'm gonna be late for lunch. Thanks!"

They watch her go, and then Frankie and Jimmy turn back to Lenny. "It's two on one. I like those odds, old-timer."

Lenny reaches into his pants pocket and comes out with a flick knife. Engraved on its silver side are the only two words of Latin these boys understand: *Semper Fi.* His gnarled hand does a limber trick and presto, there's a six-inch blade glittering in the sunlight. "Now it's two on two."

Frankie takes off across the parking lot, Jimmy right behind him.

18

"IMAGINE THAT, GWENDY WINS again," Sallie says, rolling her eyes and tossing her cards onto the carpet in front of her.

There are four of them sitting in a circle on the Peterson's den floor: Gwendy, Sallie Ackerman, Brigette Desjardin, and Josie Wainwright. The other three girls are seniors at Castle Rock High and frequent visitors to the Peterson home this school year.

"You ever notice that?" Josie says, scrunching up her face. "Gwendy never loses. At pretty much anything."

Sallie rolls with it: "Best grades in school. Best athlete in school. Prettiest girl in school. And a card shark to boot."

"Oh, shut up," Gwendy says, gathering the cards. It's her turn to shuffle and deal. "That's not true."

But Gwendy knows it is true, and although Josie is just teasing in her usual goofy way (who else would aspire to be lead singer in a group called the Pussycats?), she also knows that Sallie isn't teasing at all. Sallie is getting sick of it. Sallie is getting jealous.

Gwendy first realized it was becoming an issue a few months earlier. Yes, she's a fast runner, maybe the fastest varsity runner in the county. Maybe in the entire state. Really? Yes, really. And then there are her grades. She always earned good ones in school, but in younger years she had to study hard for those grades, and even then, there were usually a handful of B's, along with all those A's on her report cards. Now she barely hits the books at all, and her grades are the highest in the whole junior class. She even finds herself writing down the wrong answers from time to time, just to avoid, ho-hum, another perfect test score. Or forcing herself to lose at cards and arcade games just to keep her friends from becoming suspicious. Regardless of her efforts, they know something is weird anyway.

Buttons aside, coins aside, little chocolate treats aside, the box has given her...well...*powers.*

Really? Yes, really.

She never gets hurt anymore. No strained muscles from track. No bumps or bruises from soccer. No nicks or scratches from being clumsy. Not even a stubbed toe or broken fingernail. She can't remember the last time she's needed a Band-Aid. Even her period is easy. No more cramps, a few drops on a sanitary pad, and done. These days Gwendy's blood stays where it belongs.

These realizations are both fascinating and terrifying to Gwendy. She knows it's the box somehow doing this—or perhaps the chocolate treats—but they really are one and the same. Sometimes, she wishes she could talk to someone about it. Sometimes, she wishes she were still friends with Olive. She might be the only person in the world who would listen and believe her.

Gwendy places the deck of cards on the floor and gets to her feet. "Who wants popcorn and lemonade?"

Three hands go up. Gwendy disappears into the kitchen.

RICHARD CHIZMAR

19

THERE ARE BIG CHANGES in Gwendy's life during the fall and winter of 1978, most of them good ones.

She finally gets her driver's license in late September, and a month later on her seventeenth birthday, her parents surprise her with a gently used Ford Fiesta from the dealership where her mom works. The car is bright orange and the radio only works when it wants to, but none of that matters to Gwendy. She loves this car and plasters its meager back deck with big daisy decals and a NO NUKES bumper sticker left over from the sixties.

She also gets her first real job (she's earned money in the past babysitting and raking leaves, but she doesn't count those), working at the drive-in snack bar three nights a week. It surprises no one that she proves especially adept at her duties and earns a promotion by her third month of employment.

She is also named captain of the varsity outdoor track team.

Gwendy still wonders about Mr. Farris and she still worries about the button box, but not nearly with the same nervous intensity as she once did. She also still locks her bedroom door and slides the box out from inside her closet and pulls the lever for a chocolate treat, but not as often as she once did. Maybe twice a week now, tops.

In fact, she's finally relaxed to the point where she actually finds herself wondering one afternoon: *Do you think you might eventually just forget about it?*

But then she stumbles upon a newspaper article about the accidental release of anthrax spores at a Soviet bioweapons facility that killed hundreds of people and threatened the countryside, and she knows that she will never forget about the box and its red button and the responsibility she has taken on. Exactly what responsibility is that? She's not sure, but thinks it might be to just keep things from, well, getting out of hand. It sounds crazy, but feels just about right.

Near the end of her junior year, in March 1979, Gwendy watches television coverage of the nuclear meltdown at Three Mile Island in Pennsylvania. She becomes obsessed, combing over all the coverage she can find, mainly to determine how much of a danger the accident poses to surrounding communities and cities and states. The idea worries her.

She tells herself she will press the red button again if she has to and make Three Mile go away. Only Jonestown weighs heavy on her mind. Was that crazy religious fuck going to do it anyway, or did she somehow push him into it? Were the nurses going to poison those babies anyway, or did Gwendy Peterson somehow give them the extra crazy they needed to do it? What if the button box is like the monkey's paw in that story? What if it makes things worse instead of better? What if *she* makes things worse?

With Jonestown, I didn't understand. Now I do. And isn't that why Mr. Farris trusted me with the box in the first place? To do the right thing when the time came?

When the situation at Three Mile Island is finally contained and subsequent studies prove there is no further danger, Gwendy is overjoyed—and relieved. She feels like she's dodged a bullet.

20

THE FIRST THING GWENDY notices when she strolls into Castle Rock High on the last Thursday morning of the school year are the somber expressions on the faces of several teachers and a cluster of girls gathered by the cafeteria doors, many of them crying.

"What's going on?" she asks Josie Wainwright at the locker they share.

"What do you mean?"

"Kids are crying in the lobby. Everyone looks upset."

"Oh, that," Josie says, with no more gravity than if she were talking about what she'd eaten for breakfast that morning. "Some girl killed herself last night. Jumped off the Suicide Stairs."

Gwendy's entire body goes cold.

"What girl?" Barely a whisper, because she's afraid she already knows the answer. She doesn't know how she knows, but she does.

"Olive...uhh..."

"Kepnes. Her name is Olive Kepnes."

"*Was* Olive Kepnes," Josie says, and starts humming "The Dead March."

Gwendy wants to smack her, right in her pretty freckled face, but she can't lift her arms. Her entire body is numb. After a moment, she wills her legs to move and walks out of the school and to her car. She drives directly home and locks herself inside her bedroom.

21

IT'S MY FAULT, GWENDY thinks for the hundredth time, as she pulls her car into the Castle View Recreational Park parking lot. It's almost midnight and the gravel lot is empty. *If I'd stayed her friend...*

She's told her parents that she's sleeping over at Maggie Bean's house with a bunch of girlfriends from school—all of them telling stories and reminiscing about Olive and supporting each other in their grief—and her parents believe her. They don't understand that Gwendy stopped running with Olive's crowd a long time ago. Most of the girls Gwendy hangs out with now wouldn't recognize Olive if she were standing in front of them. Other than a quick "Hey" in the hallways at school or the occasional encounter at the supermarket, Gwendy hasn't spoken to Olive in probably six or seven months. They eventually made up after their fight in Gwendy's bedroom, but nothing had been the same since that day. And the truth of the matter is that had been okay with Gwendy. Olive was getting to be too damn sensitive, too high maintenance, just…too *Olive*.

"It's my fault," Gwendy mutters as she gets out of the car. She'd like to believe that's just adolescent angst—what her father calls Teenage It's All About Me Complex—but she can't quite get there. Can't help realizing that if she and Olive had stayed tight, the girl would still be alive.

There's no moon in the sky tonight and she forgot to bring along a flashlight, but that doesn't matter to Gwendy. She strikes off in the dark at a brisk pace and heads for the Suicide Stairs, unsure of what she's going to do once she gets there.

She's halfway across the park before she realizes she doesn't want to go to the Suicide Stairs at all. In fact, she never wants to see them again. Because— this is crazy, but in the dark it has the force of truth—what if she met Olive halfway up? Olive with her head half bashed in and one eye dangling on her cheek? What if Olive pushed her? Or talked her into jumping?

Gwendy turns around, climbs back into her cute little Fiesta, and drives home. It occurs to her that she can make damn sure no one jumps from those stairs again.

22

The Castle Rock Call

Saturday edition—May 26, 1979

Sometime between the hours of one a.m. and six a.m. on the morning of Friday, May 25, a portion of the Northeastern corner of the Castle View Recreational Park was destroyed. The historic stairway and viewing platform, as well as nearly one-half acre of state-owned property, collapsed, leaving a bewildering pile of iron, steel, earth, and rubble below.

Numerous authorities are still on site investigating the scene to determine if the collapse was a result of natural or man-made causes.

"It's just the strangest thing, and way too early for answers," Castle Rock Sheriff George

Bannerman commented. "We don't know if there was a minor earthquake centered in this area or if someone somehow sabotaged the stairs or what. We're bringing in additional investigators from Portland, but they're not expected to arrive until tomorrow morning, so it's best we wait until that time to make any further announcements."

Castle View was recently the scene of tragedy when the body of a seventeen-year-old female was discovered at the base of the cliff...

23

GWENDY IS SICK FOR days afterward. Mr. and Mrs. Peterson believe grief is causing their daughter's fever and upset stomach, but Gwendy knows better. It's the box. It's the price she has to pay for pushing the red button. She heard the rumble of the collapsing rocks, and had to run into the bathroom and vomit.

She manages to shower and change out of baggy sweatpants and a t-shirt long enough to attend Olive's funeral on Monday morning, but only after her mother's prompting. If it were up to Gwendy, she wouldn't have left her bedroom. Maybe not until she was twenty-four or so.

The church is SRO. Most of Castle Rock High School is there—teachers and students alike; even Frankie Stone is there, smirking in the back pew—and

121

Gwendy hates them all for showing up. None of them even liked Olive when she was alive. None of them even *knew* her.

Yeah, like I *did,* Gwendy thinks. *But at least I did something about it. There's that. No one else will jump from those stairs. Ever.*

Walking from the gravesite back to her parents' car after the service, someone calls out to her. She turns and sees Olive's father.

Mr. Kepnes is a short man, barrel-chested, with rosy cheeks and kind eyes. Gwendy has always adored him and shared a special bond with Olive's father, perhaps because they once shared the burden of being overweight, or perhaps because Mr. Kepnes is one of the sweetest people Gwendy has ever known.

She held it together pretty well during the funeral service, but now, with Olive's father approaching, arms outstretched, Gwendy loses it and begins to sob.

"It's okay, honey," Mr. Kepnes says, wrapping her up in a bear hug. "It's okay."

Gwendy vehemently shakes her head. "It's not..." Her face is a mess of tears and snot. She wipes it with her sleeve.

"Listen to me." Mr. Kepnes leans down and makes sure Gwendy is looking at him. It's wrong for the father to be comforting the friend—the *ex*-friend—

but that is exactly what he's doing. "It has to be okay. I know it doesn't feel like it right now, but it *has* to be. Got it?"

Gwendy nods her head and whispers, "Got it." She just wants to go home.

"You were her best friend in the world, Gwendy. Maybe in a couple weeks, you can come see us at the house. We can all sit down and have some lunch and talk. I think Olive would've liked that."

It's too much, and Gwendy can no longer bear it. She pulls away and flees for the car, her apologetic parents trailing behind her.

The final two days of school are canceled because of the tragedy. Gwendy spends most of the next week on the den sofa buried beneath a blanket. She has many bad dreams—the worst of them featuring a man in a black suit and black hat, shiny silver coins where his eyes should be—and often cries out in her sleep. She's afraid of what she might say during these nightmares. She's afraid her parents might overhear.

Eventually, the fever breaks and Gwendy reenters the world. She spends the majority of her summer vacation working as much as she can at the snack bar. When she's not working, she's jogging the sunbaked roads of Castle Rock or locked inside her bedroom listening to music. Anything to keep her mind busy.

The button box stays hidden in the back of the closet. Gwendy still thinks about it—boy, does she— but she wants nothing to do with it anymore. Not the chocolate treats, not the silver coins, and most of all, not the goddamn buttons. Most days, she hates the box and everything it reminds her of, and she fantasizes about getting rid of it. Crushing it with a sledge-hammer or wrapping it up in a blanket and driving it out to the dump.

But she knows she can't do that. *What if someone else finds it? What if someone else pushes one of the buttons?*

She leaves it there in the dark shadows of her closet, growing cobwebs and gathering dust. *Let the damn thing rot for all I care,* she thinks.

24

GWENDY IS SUNBATHING IN the back yard, listening to Bob Seger & the Silver Bullet Band on a Sony Walkman, when Mrs. Peterson comes outside carrying a glass of ice water. Her mother hands Gwendy the glass and sits down on the end of the lawn chair.

"You doing okay, honey?"

Gwendy slips off the headphones and takes a drink. "I'm fine."

Mrs. Peterson gives her a look.

"Okay, maybe not fine, but I'm doing better."

"I hope so." She gives Gwendy's leg a squeeze. "You know we're here if you ever want to talk. About anything."

"I know."

"You're just so quiet all the time. We worry about you."

"I…have a lot on my mind."

"Still not ready to call Mr. Kepnes back?"

Gwendy doesn't answer, only shakes her head.

Mrs. Peterson gets up from the lawn chair. "Just remember one thing."

"What's that?"

"It will get better. It always does."

It's pretty much what Olive's father said. Gwendy hopes it's true, but she has her doubts.

"Hey, mom?"

Mrs. Peterson stops and turns around.

"I love you."

25

As it turns out, Mr. Kepnes was wrong and Mrs. Peterson was right. Things are not okay, but they do get better.

Gwendy meets a boy.

His name is Harry Streeter. He's eighteen years old, tall and handsome and funny. He's new to Castle Rock (his family just moved in a couple weeks ago as a result of his father's job transfer), and if it's not a genuine case of Love At First Sight, it's pretty close.

Gwendy is behind the counter at the snack bar, hustling tubs of buttered popcorn, Laffy Taffy, Pop Rocks, and soda by the gallon, when Harry walks in with his younger brother. She notices him right away, and he notices her. When it's his turn to order, the spark jumps and neither of them can manage a complete sentence.

Harry returns the next night, by himself this time, even though *The Amityville Horror* and *Phantasm* are still playing, and once again he waits his turn in line. This time, along with a small popcorn and soda, he asks Gwendy for her phone number.

He calls the next afternoon, and that evening picks her up in a candy-apple red Mustang convertible. With his blond hair and blue eyes, he looks like a movie star. They go bowling and have pizza on their first date, skating at the Gates Falls Roller Rink on their second, and after that they are inseparable. Picnics at Castle Lake, day trips into Portland to visit museums and the big shopping mall, movies, walks. They even jog together, keeping in perfect step.

By the time school starts, Gwendy is wearing Harry's school ring on a silver chain around her neck and trying to figure out how to talk to her mother about birth control. (This talk won't happen until the school year is almost two months old, but when it does, Gwendy is relieved to find that her mother is not only understanding, she even calls and makes the doctor's appointment for her—go, Mom.)

There are other changes, too. Much to the dismay of the coaching staff and her teammates, Gwendy decides to skip her senior season on the girls' soccer team. Her heart just isn't in it. Besides, Harry isn't a jock, he's a serious photographer, and this way they can spend more time together.

Gwendy can't remember ever being this happy. The button box still surfaces in her thoughts from time to time, but it's almost as if the whole thing was a dream from her childhood. *Mr. Farris. The chocolate treats. The silver dollars. The red button. Was any of it real?*

Running, however, is not negotiable. When indoor track season rolls around in late November, Gwendy is ready to rock and roll. Harry is there on the sidelines for every meet, snapping pix and cheering her on. Despite training most of the summer and into the fall, Gwendy finishes a disappointing fourth in Counties and doesn't qualify for States for the first time in her high school career. She also brings home two B's on her semester-ending report card in December. On the third morning of Christmas break, Gwendy wakes up and shuffles to the hallway bathroom to take her morning pee. When she's finished, she uses her right foot to slide the scale out from underneath the bathroom vanity, and she steps onto it. Her instincts are right: she has gained six pounds.

26

GWENDY'S FIRST IMPULSE IS to sprint down the hallway, lock her bedroom door, and yank out the button box so she can pull the small lever and devour a magic chocolate treat. She can almost hear the voices chanting in her head: *Goodyear! Goodyear! Goodyear!*

But she doesn't do that.

Instead, she closes the toilet lid and sits back down. *Let's see, I bombed my track season, pulled a pair of B's for the semester (one of them just barely a B, although her parents don't know that), and I gained weight (six whole pounds!) for the first time in years—and I'm still the happiest I've ever been.*

I don't need it, she thinks. *More importantly, I don't want it.* The realization makes her head sing and her heart soar, and Gwendy returns to her bedroom with a spring to her step and a smile on her face.

27

THE NEXT MORNING, GWENDY wakes up on the floor of her closet.

She's cradling the button box in her arms like a faithful lover and her right thumb is resting a half-inch from the black button.

She stifles a scream and jerks her hand away, scrambling like a crab out of the closet. A safe distance away, she gets to her feet and notices something that makes her head swim: the narrow wooden shelf on the button box is standing open. On it is a tiny chocolate treat: a parrot, every feather perfect.

Gwendy wants more than anything to run from the room, slam the door behind her, and never return—but she knows she can't do that. So what *can* she do?

She approaches the button box with as much stealth as she can muster. When she's within a few feet of it, the image of a wild animal asleep in its lair flashes in her head, and she thinks: *The button box doesn't just give power; it* is *power.*

"But I won't," she mutters. *Won't what?* "Won't give in."

Before she can chicken out, she lunges and snatches the piece of chocolate from the little shelf. She backs out of the bedroom, afraid to turn her back on the button box, hurries down the hall into the bathroom, where she hurls the chocolate parrot into the toilet and flushes it away.

And for a while, everything is all right. She thinks the button box goes to sleep, but she doesn't trust that, not a bit. Because even if it does, it sleeps with one eye open.

28

TWO LIFE-CHANGING EVENTS OCCUR at the start of Gwendy's final semester of high school: her college application to study psychology at Brown University is granted an early acceptance, and she sleeps with Harry for the first time.

There've been several false starts over the past few months—Gwendy has been on the pill for at least that long—but each time she isn't quite ready, and gallant Harry Streeter doesn't pressure her. The deed finally goes down in Harry's candlelit bedroom on the Friday night of his father's big work party, and it is every bit as awkward and wonderful as expected. To make the necessary improvements, Gwendy and Harry do it again the next two nights in the back seat of Harry's Mustang. It's cramped back there, but it only gets better.

Gwendy runs outdoor track again when spring comes, and places in the top three in her first two meets. Her grades are currently A's across the board (although History is hovering in the danger zone at 91%), and she hasn't stepped on a scale since the week before Christmas. She's done with that nonsense.

She still suffers from the occasional nightmare (the one featuring the well-dressed man with the silver coin eyes continuing to be the most terrifying), and she still knows the button box wants her back, but she tries not to dwell on that. Most days she is successful, thanks to Harry and what she thinks of as her new life. She often daydreams that Mr. Farris will return to take back possession of the button box, relieving her of the responsibility. Or that the box will eventually forget about her. That would sound stupid to an outsider, but Gwendy has come to believe that the box is in some way alive.

Only there will be no forgetting. She discovers this on a breezy spring afternoon in April, while she and Harry are flying a kite in the outfield of the Castle Rock High baseball field (Gwendy was delighted when he showed up at her house with the kite in tow). She notices something small and dark emerge from the tree-line bordering the school property. At first she thinks it's an animal of some sort. A bunny or perhaps

a woodchuck on the move. But as it gets closer—and it seems to head directly at them—she realizes that it's not an animal at all. It's a hat.

Harry is holding the spool of string and staring up at the red, white, and blue kite with wide eyes and a smile on his face. He doesn't notice the black hat coming in their direction, not moving with the wind but against it. He doesn't notice the hat slow down as it approaches, then suddenly change direction and swoop a complete circle around his horrorstruck girl-friend—almost as if kissing her hello, so nice to see you again—before it skitters off and disappears behind the bleachers that run alongside the third base line.

Harry notices none of these things because it's a gorgeous spring afternoon in Castle Rock and he's fly-ing a kite with the love of his young life at his side, and everything is perfect.

29

THE FIRST HALF OF May passes in a blur of classes, tests, and graduation planning. Everything from sizing caps and gowns, to sending out commencement notices in the mail, to finalizing graduation night party arrangements. Final exams are scheduled for the week of May 19th and the Castle Rock High School graduation ceremony will take place on the football field the following Tuesday, the 27th.

For Gwendy and Harry, everything is set. After the ceremony is finished, they will change clothes and head to Brigette Desjardin's house for the biggest and best graduation party in the school. The next morning, they leave for a week-long camping trip to Casco Bay, just the two of them. Once they return home, it will be work at the drive-in for Gwendy and at the hardware store for Harry. In early August, a ten-day vacation at the coast with Harry's family. After that, it's on to college (Brown for Gwendy; nearby Providence for Harry) and an exciting new chapter in their lives. They can't wait.

Gwendy knows she will have to make a decision about what to do with the button box once it's time to leave for college, but that's months in the future, and it's not a priority this evening. The biggest decision facing Gwendy at the moment is which dress to wear to Brigette's party.

"Good lord," Harry says, smiling. "Just pick one, already. Or go as you are." *As she is* happens to be in bra and panties.

Gwendy gives him a poke in the ribs and turns to the next page in the catalog. "Easy for you to say, mister. You'll put on jeans and a t-shirt and look like a million bucks."

"You look like a *trillion* in your underwear."

They're lying on their stomachs on Gwendy's bed. Harry is toying with her hair; Gwendy is paging through the glossy Brown catalogue. Mr. and Mrs. Peterson are at dinner with neighbors down the block and not expected back until late. Gwendy and Harry came in an hour ago, and Gwendy was mildly surprised to find she didn't need to use her key. The front door was not only unlocked but slightly ajar. (Her dad is big on locking up; likes to say Castle Rock isn't the little country town it used to be.) But everyone forgets stuff, plus Dad's not getting any younger. And with thoughts of the party to occupy them—not to mention thirty minutes of heaven in her bed beforehand—neither notices a few splinters sticking out around the lock. Or the pry marks.

"C'mon," Harry says now, "you're a knockout. It doesn't matter what you wear."

"I just can't decide whether to go strapless and dressy or long and flowy and summery." She tosses the catalog on the floor and gets up. "Here, I'll let you choose." She walks to the closet, opens the door…and smells him before she sees him: beer, cigarettes, and sweat-funk.

She starts to turn around and call to Harry, but she's too late. A pair of strong arms reach out from the shadows and hanging clothes and pull her to the floor. Now she finds her voice, "Harry!"

He's already off the bed and moving. He hurls himself at Gwendy's attacker, and amidst a tangle of clothes hangers and blouses, they grapple across the floor.

Gwendy pushes herself back up against the wall and is stunned to see Frankie Stone, dressed in camo pants, dark glasses, and t-shirt, as if he thinks he's a soldier on a secret mission, rolling around her bedroom floor with her boyfriend. That's bad, but something else is worse: lying on the closet floor, half-buried in fallen clothes, is a scatter of silver dollars…and the button box. Frankie must have found it while he was waiting for her, or while he was waiting for Harry to leave.

Has he pushed any of the buttons?

Is Africa gone? Or Europe?

The two young men crash into the night table. Hairbrushes and makeup rain down on them. Frankie's Secret Agent Man shades fly off. Harry outweighs Frankie by at least thirty pounds, and pins the skinny little dipshit to the floor. "Gwen?" He sounds perfectly calm. "Call the police. I've got this skanky little motherf—"

But that's when it all goes to hell. Frankie is skinny, Frankie doesn't have much in the way of muscles, but that is also true of snakes. He moves like a snake now, first wriggling, then hoisting one knee into the crotch of Harry's boxers. Harry makes an *ooof* sound and tilts forward. Frankie pulls one hand free, makes finger-prongs, and jabs them into Harry's eyes. Harry screams, claps a hand to his face, and falls to one side.

Gwendy pushes herself up in time to see Frankie coming at her, grabbing for her with one hand and trying to get something out of the pocket of his camo pants with the other. Before he can touch her, Harry tackles him and they go reeling into the closet, falling and pulling down more dresses and skirts and pants and tops, so at first Gwendy can see nothing but a pile of clothes that appears to be breathing.

Then a hand emerges—a dirty hand with blue webbing tattooed across the back. It paws around aimlessly at first, then finds the button box. Gwendy tries to scream, but nothing comes out; her throat is locked tight. The box comes down corner first. Once...then twice...then three times. The first time it connects with Harry's head, the sound is muffled by clothes. The second time it's louder. The third time, the hit produces a sickening crack, like a breaking branch, and the corner of the box is coated with blood and hair.

The clothes heave and slide. Frankie emerges, still holding the button box in one tattooed hand. He's grinning. Behind him she can see Harry. His eyes are closed, his mouth hangs open.

"Don't know what this is, pretty girl, but it hits real good."

She darts past him. He doesn't try to stop her. She goes on her knees beside Harry and lifts his head with one hand. She cups the other palm in front of his nose and mouth, but she already knows. The box used to be light, but for a while tonight it was heavy, because it *wanted* to be heavy. Frankie Stone has used it to crush the top of Harry Streeter's skull. There is no breath on her palm.

"You killed him! You filthy son of a bitch, *you killed him!*"

"Yeah, well, maybe. Whatever." He seems uninterested in the dead boy; his eyes are busily crawling over Gwendy's body, and she understands he's crazy. A box that can destroy the world is in the hands of a crazy person who thinks he's a Green Beret or a Navy SEAL or something like that. "What is this thing? Besides where you store your silver dollars, that is? How much are they worth, Gwennie? And what do these buttons do?"

He touches the green one, then the violet one, and as his grimy thumb moves toward the black one, Gwendy does the only thing she can think of. Only she doesn't think, she just acts. Her bra closes in front, and now she opens it. "Do you want to play with those buttons, or with mine?"

Frankie grins, exposing teeth that would make even a hardened dentist wince and turn away. He reaches into his pocket again, and pulls out a knife. It reminds her of Lenny's, except there's no *Semper Fi* engraved on it. "Get over on the bed, Prom Queen. Don't bother taking off your panties. I want to cut them off you. If you lay real still, maybe I won't cut what's underneath."

"Did he send you?" Gwendy asks. She's sitting on her bottom now, with her feet on the floor and her legs drawn up to hide her breasts. With luck, one look at them is all this sick bastard is going to get. "Did Mr. Farris send you to take the box? Did he want *you* to have it?" Although the evidence seems to point to this, it's hard to believe.

He's frowning. "Mr. *who?*"

"Farris. Black suit? Little black hat that goes wherever it wants to?"

"I don't know any Mr. F—"

That's when she lashes out, once again not thinking...although later it will occur to her that the *box* might have been thinking for her. His eyes widen and the hand holding the knife pistons forward, driving through her foot and coming out the other side in a bouquet of blood. She shrieks as her heel slams into Frankie's chest, driving him back into the closet. She snatches up the box, and at the same time she pushes the red button, she screams, *"Rot in hell!"*

30

GWENDY PETERSON GRADUATES FROM Brown *summa cum laude* in June of 1984. There has been no running track for her since her senior spring in high school; the knife-wound in her foot got infected while she was in the hospital, and although it cleared eventually, she lost a piece of it. She still walks with a limp, although now it is barely discernable.

She goes out to dinner with her parents after the ceremony, and they have a fine time. Mr. and Mrs. Peterson even break their long abstinence with a bottle of champagne to toast their daughter, who is bound for Columbia grad school, or—perhaps—the Iowa Writers' Workshop. She thinks she might have a novel in her. Maybe more than one.

"And is there a man in your life?" Mrs. Peterson asks. Her color is high and her eyes are bright from the unaccustomed alcohol.

Gwendy shakes her head, smiling. "No man currently."

Nor, she thinks, will there be in the future. She already has a significant other; it's a box with eight buttons on top and two levers on the side. She still eats the occasional chocolate, but she hasn't taken one of the silver dollars in years. The ones she did have are gone, parceled out one or two at a time for books, rent (oh God, the luxury of a single apartment), and an upgrade from the Fiesta to a Subaru Outback (which outraged her mother, but she got over it eventually).

"Well," says Mr. Peterson, "there's time for that."

"Yes." Gwendy smiles. "I have plenty of time."

31

SHE'S GOING TO SPEND the summer in Castle Rock, so when her parents have gone back to their hotel, she packs up the last of her things, stowing the button box at the very bottom of her trunk. During her time at Brown, she kept the awful thing in a safe deposit box in the Bank of Rhode Island, something she wishes she had thought of doing sooner, but she was just a kid when she got it, a *kid*, goddammit, and what do kids know? Kids stow valuables in cavities under trees, or behind loose stones in cellars prone to flooding, or in closets. In *closets*, for Christ's sake! Once she gets to Columbia (or Iowa City, if the Writers' Workshop accepts her), it will go into another safety deposit box, and as far as she's concerned, it can stay there forever.

She decides to have a slice of coffee cake and a glass of milk before going to bed. She gets as far as the living room, and there she stops cold. Sitting on the desk where she has attended to her studies for the last two years, next to a framed picture of Harry Streeter, is a small, neat black hat. She has no doubt that it's the one she last saw on the day she and Harry were flying that kite on the baseball field. Such a happy day that was. Maybe the last happy one.

"Come on out here, Gwendy," Mr. Farris calls from the kitchen. "Set a spell, as they say down south."

She walks into the kitchen, feeling like a visitor in her own body. Mr. Farris, in his neat black suit and not looking a day older, sits at the kitchen table. He has a piece of the coffee cake and a glass of milk. Her own cake and milk are waiting for her.

He looks her up and down, but—as on that day ten years ago when she first met him at the top of the Suicide Stairs—without salacious intent. "What a fine young woman you've grown into, Gwendy Peterson!"

She doesn't thank him for the compliment, but she sits down. To her, this conversation seems long overdue. Probably not to him; she has an idea that Mr. Farris has his own schedule, and he always stays on it. What she says is, "I locked up when I went out. I always lock up. And the door was still locked when I came back. I always make sure. That's a habit I got into on the day Harry died. Do you know about Harry? If you knew I wanted coffee cake and milk, I suppose you do."

"Of course. I know a great deal about you, Gwendy. As for the locks…" He waves it aside, as if to say *pish-tush*.

"Have you come for the box?" She hears both eagerness and reluctance in her voice. A strange combination, but one she knows quite well.

He ignores this, at least for the time being. "As I said, I know a great deal about you, but I don't know exactly what happened on the day the Stone kid came to your house. There's always a crisis with the button box—a moment of truth, one could say—and when it comes, my ability to…see…is lost. Tell me what happened."

"Do I have to?"

He raises a hand and turns it over, as if to say *Up to you.*

"I've never told anyone."

"And never will, would be my guess. This is your one chance."

"I said I hoped he'd rot in hell, and I pushed the red button at the same time. I didn't mean it literally, but he'd just killed the boy I loved, he'd just stuck a knife right through my fucking foot, and it was what came out. I never thought he'd actually..."

Only he did.

She falls silent, remembering how Frankie's face began to turn black, how his eyes first went cloudy and then lolled forward in their sockets. How his mouth drooped, the lower lip unrolling like a shade with a broken spring. His scream—surprise? agony? both? she doesn't know—that blew the teeth right out of his putrefying gums in a shower of yellow and black. His jaw tearing loose; his chin falling all the way down to his chest; the ghastly ripping sound his neck made when it tore open. The rivers of pus from his cheeks as they pulled apart like rotting sailcloth—

"I don't know if he rotted in hell, but he certainly rotted," Gwendy says. She pushes away the coffee cake. She no longer wants it.

"What was your story?" he asks. "Tell me that. You must have thought remarkably fast."

"I don't know if I did or not. I've always wondered if the box did the thinking for me."

She waits for him to respond. He doesn't, so she goes on.

"I closed my eyes and pushed the red button again while I imagined Frankie gone. I concentrated on that as hard as I could, and when I opened my eyes, only

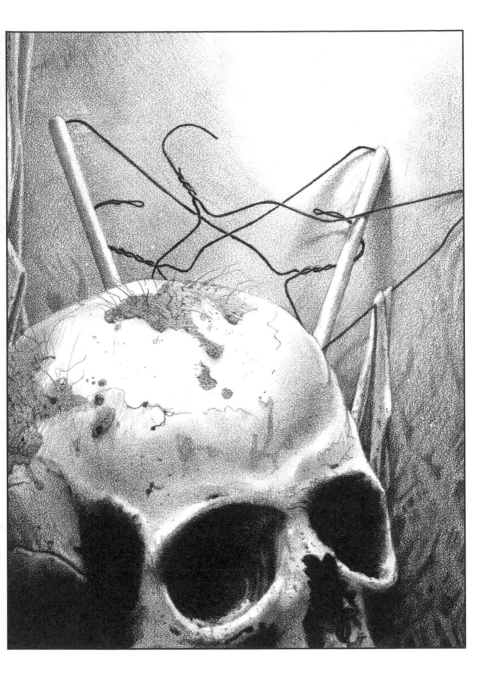

Harry was in the closet." She shakes her head wonderingly. "It worked."

"Of course it worked," Mr. Farris says. "The red button is very...versatile, shall we say? Yes, let's say that. But in ten years you only pushed it a few times, showing you to be a person of strong will and stronger restraint. I salute you for that." And he actually does, with his glass of milk.

"Even once was too much," she says. "I caused Jonestown."

"You give yourself far too much credit," he says sharply. "*Jim Jones* caused Jonestown. The so-called Reverend was as crazy as a rat in a rainbarrel. Paranoid, mother-fixated, and full of deadly conceit. As for your friend Olive, I know you've always felt you were somehow responsible for her suicide, but I assure you that's not the case. Olive had ISSUES. Your word for it."

She stares at him, amazed. How much of her life has he been peering into, like a pervert (Frankie Stone, for instance) going through her underwear drawer?

"One of those issues was her stepfather. He...how shall I put it? He *fiddled* with her."

"Are you serious?"

"As a heart attack. And you know the truth about young Mr. Stone."

She does. The police tied him to at least four other rapes and two attempted rapes in the Castle Rock area. Perhaps also to the rape-murder of a girl in Cleaves Mills. The cops are less sure about that one, but Gwendy's positive it was him.

"Stone was fixated on you for *years*, Gwendy, and he got exactly what he deserved. He was responsible for the death of your Mr. Streeter, not the button box."

She barely hears this. She's remembering what she usually banishes from her mind. Except in dreams, when she can't. "I told the police that Harry kept Frankie from raping me, that they fought, that Harry was killed and Frankie ran away. I suppose they're still looking for him. I hid the box in my dresser, along with the coins. I thought about dipping one of my high heel shoes in Harry's blood to explain the...the bludgeoning...but I couldn't bring myself to do it. In the end it didn't matter. They just assumed Frankie took the murder weapon with him."

Mr. Farris nods. "It's far from a case of all's well that ends well, but as well as can be, at least."

Gwendy's face breaks into a bitter smile that makes her look years older than twenty-two. "You make it all sound so good. As if I were Saint Gwendy. I know better. If you hadn't given me that goddamn box, things would have been different."

"If Lee Harvey Oswald hadn't gotten a job at the Texas Book Depository, Kennedy would have finished out his term," Mr. Farris says. "You can *if* things until you go crazy, my girl."

"Spin it any way you want, Mr. Farris, but if you'd never given me that box, Harry would still be alive. And Olive."

He considers. "Harry? Yes, maybe. *Maybe.* Olive, however, was doomed. You bear no responsibility for her, believe me." He smiles. "And good news! You're going to be accepted at Iowa! Your first novel..." He grins. "Well, let that be a surprise. I'll only say that you'll want to wear your prettiest dress when you pick up your award."

"What award?" She is both surprised and a little disgusted at how greedy she is for this news.

He once more waves his hand in that *pish-tush* gesture. "I've said enough. Any more, and I'll bend the course of your future, so please don't tempt me. I might give in if you did, because I like you, Gwendy. Your proprietorship of the box has been...exceptional. I know the burden it's been, sometimes like carrying an invisible packsack full of rocks on your back, but you will never know the good you've done. The disasters you've averted. When used with bad intent—which you never did, by the way, even your experiment with

Guyana was done out of simple curiosity—the box has an unimaginable capacity for evil. When left alone, it can be a strong force for good."

"My parents were on the way to alcoholism," Gwendy says. "Looking back on it, I'm almost sure of that. But they stopped drinking."

"Yes, and who knows how many worse things the box might have prevented during your proprietorship? Not even I know. Mass slaughters? A dirty suitcase bomb planted in Grand Central Station? The assassination of a leader that might have sparked World War III? It hasn't stopped everything—we both read the newspapers—but I'll tell you one thing, Gwendy." He leans forward, pinning her with his eyes. "It has stopped a lot. A *lot*."

"And now?"

"Now I'll thank you to give me the button box. Your work is done—at least that part of your work is done. You still have many things to tell the world… and the world will listen. You will entertain people, which is the greatest gift a man or woman can have. You'll make them laugh, cry, gasp, *think*. By the time you're thirty-five, you'll have a computer to write on instead of a typewriter, but both are button boxes of a kind, wouldn't you say? You will live a long life—"

"*How* long?" Again she feels that mixture of greed and reluctance.

"That I will not tell you, only that you will die surrounded by friends, in a pretty nightgown with blue flowers on the hem. There will be sun shining in your window, and before you pass you will look out and see a squadron of birds flying south. A final image of the world's beauty. There will be a little pain. Not much."

He takes a bite of his coffee cake, then stands.

"Very tasty, but I'm already late for my next appointment. The box, please."

"Who gets it next? Or can you not tell me that, either?"

"Not sure. I have my eye on a boy in a little town called Pescadero, about an hour south of San Francisco. You will never meet him. I hope, Gwendy, he's as good a custodian as you have been."

He bends toward her and kisses her on the cheek. The touch of his lips makes her happy, the way the little chocolate animals always did.

"It's at the bottom of my trunk," Gwendy says. "In the bedroom. The trunk's not locked…although I guess that wouldn't cause you any problems even if it was." She laughs, then sobers. "I just…I don't want to touch it again, or even look at it. Because if I did…"

He's smiling, but his eyes are grave. "If you did, you might want to keep it."

"Yes."

"Sit here, then. Finish your coffee cake. It really is good."

He leaves her.

32

GWENDY SITS. SHE EATS her coffee cake in small slow
bites, washing each one down with a tiny sip of milk.
She hears the squeak her trunk lid makes when it goes
up. She hears the squeak when the lid is lowered again.
She hears the *snap-snap* of the latches being consider-
ately closed. She hears his footsteps approach the door
to the hall, and pause there. Will he say goodbye?

He does not. The door opens and softly closes. Mr.
Richard Farris, first encountered on a bench at the
top of Castle View's Suicide Stairs, has left her life.
Gwendy sits for another minute, finishing the last bite
of her cake and thinking of a book she wants to write,
a sprawling saga about a small town in Maine, one
very much like her own. There will be love and horror. She isn't ready yet, but she thinks the time will

come quite soon; two years, five at most. Then she will sit down at her typewriter—her button box—and start tapping away.

At last, she gets up and walks into the living room. There's a spring in her step. Already she feels lighter. The small black hat is no longer on her desk, but he's left her something, anyway: an 1891 Morgan silver dollar. She picks it up, turning it this way and that so its uncirculated surface can catch the light. Then she laughs and puts it in her pocket.

ABOUT THE AUTHORS

STEPHEN KING IS THE author of more than fifty books, all of them worldwide bestsellers. His recent work includes The Bill Hodges Trilogy, *The Bazaar of Bad Dreams*, *Revival*, *Doctor Sleep*, and *Under the Dome*. His novel *11/22/63* was named a top ten book of 2011 by *The New York Times Book Review* and won the Los Angeles Times Book Prize for Mystery/Thriller. He is the recipient of the 2014 National Medal of Arts and the 2003 National Book Foundation Medal for Distinguished Contribution to American Letters. He lives in Bangor, Maine, with his wife, novelist Tabitha King.

RICHARD CHIZMAR'S FICTION HAS appeared in dozens of publications, including *Ellery Queen's Mystery Magazine* and multiple editions of *The Year's 25 Finest Crime and Mystery Stories*. He has won two World Fantasy awards, four International Horror Guild awards, and the HWA's Board of Trustee's award. His third short story collection, *A Long December*, was recently published to starred reviews in both *Kirkus* and *Booklist*, and

STEPHEN KING

was featured in *Entertainment Weekly*. Chizmar's work has been translated into many languages throughout the world, and he has appeared at numerous conferences as a writing instructor, guest speaker, panelist, and guest of honor. Please visit the author's website at RichardChizmar.com.

ABOUT THE ARTISTS

BEN BALDWIN IS AN artist and illustrator who works with a variety of mediums from photography and digital art programs to more traditional drawing and painting techniques. He has produced book cover designs and magazine illustrations for many clients around the world as well as one-off paintings or drawings for private commissions.

KEITH MINNION SOLD HIS first short story to *Asimov's SF Adventure Magazine* in 1979. He has sold over twenty stories, two novelettes, an art book of his best published illustrations, and one novel since. Keith has illustrated professionally since the early 1990s for such writers as William Peter Blatty, Gene Wolfe, and Neil Gaiman, and has also done extensive graphic design work for the Department of Defense. He is a former school teacher, DOD program manager, and officer in the U.S. Navy. He currently lives in the Shenandoah Valley of Virginia, pursuing oil and watercolor painting, and fiction writing.